**Lose yourself in a heartrending duet
from Lucy Clark...**

SAVING TWIN BABIES

WEDDING ON THE BABY WARD

Delivering these premature conjoined twins
is neonatal specialist Miles Trevellion's
only priority—the compellingly
beautiful Dr Janessa Austen can be
nothing more than his colleague. For now...

SPECIAL CARE BABY MIRACLE

New mum Sheena's tiny girls
are fighting for their lives, and
paediatric surgeon Will Beckman is the man
to save them! Sheena's hoping for two little
miracles—but perhaps an unexpected
third dream might also come true...

SAVING TWIN BABIES

*Only the world's most renowned doctors—
and a miracle or two—
can save these tiny twins.*

**Both titles are available this month
from Mills & Boon Medical™ Romance.**

Lucy Clark is actually a husband-and-wife writing team. They enjoy taking holidays with their children, during which they discuss and develop new ideas for their books using the fantastic Australian scenery. They use their daily walks to talk over characterisation and fine details of the wonderful stories they produce, and are avid movie buffs. They live on the edge of a popular wine district in South Australia with their two children, and enjoy spending family time together at weekends.

Recent titles by the same author:

DOCTOR DIAMOND IN THE ROUGH
THE DOCTOR'S SOCIETY SWEETHEART
THE DOCTOR'S DOUBLE TROUBLE

These titles are also available in ebook format from www.millsandboon.co.uk

SPECIAL CARE BABY MIRACLE

BY
LUCY CLARK

First published in Great Britain 2011
by Mills & Boon, an imprint of Harlequin (UK) Limited.
Large Print edition 2012
Harlequin (UK) Limited, Eton House,
18-24 Paradise Road, Richmond, Surrey TW9 1SR

© Anne and Peter Clark 2011

ISBN: 978 0 263 22431 3

Harlequin (UK) policy is to use papers that are natural, renewable and recyclable products and made from wood grown in sustainable forests. The logging and manufacturing process conform to the legal environmental regulations of the country of origin.

Printed and bound in Great Britain
by CPI Antony Rowe, Chippenham, Wiltshire

Dear Reader

Babies are always so cute but beautiful twin girls who are born conjoined can really capture your heart. Ellie and Sarah are two little girls who came into the world and unbeknownst to them, ended up uniting four very special people.

Janessa and Miles were so much fun to write, especially the part about making Janessa a pilot. After being given a joy-ride flight in a tiger moth biplane as a birthday present, we knew the experience was one that needed to be relayed in a book. The airfield where Janessa flies her plane is one of our favourite places to visit and part of the book was even typed there, sipping a nice cup of coffee on a pleasant Spring day while the lovely old planes take to the skies.

Sheena and Will brought their own set of unique challenges to the story. For Sheena, going through not only the pregnancy but the long awaited separation of her gorgeous twin girls was gut wrenching to write, especially after reading and researching how parents feel when faced with such situations. With Will by her side, loving and caring for not only her but the girls as well, Sheena was able to get the happily ever after she so richly deserved.

We hope you enjoy reading about these special babies who have brought together two couples who were made for each other.

Warmest regards,

For Sheena and Will—
never 'dare' a writer! You two are awesome.
—*Pr* 23:4–5

CHAPTER ONE

THE string quartet began to play and Sheena finished fussing with her friend Janessa's bridal veil. Sheena, Kaycee and Janessa were all in a small side room next to a large aeroplane hangar.

'Only *you* would get married in an aeroplane hangar.' Kaycee, one of the nurses Sheena and Janessa had worked with for years, couldn't help but smile.

Sheena laughed, knowing it wasn't the first time Janessa had heard such a comment.

'Well…I *am* a pilot as well as a doctor. Besides, this airfield was part of my childhood. My dad loved to fly and my mum loved to watch him. Now that they're both gone, I guess I feel closest to my parents when I'm here,' Janessa replied with a nostalgic sigh.

'There.' Sheena stepped back and surveyed her closest friend. The two women were as close as sisters and today she was so proud of Janessa. 'You look radiant.' Sheena so desperately wanted everything to go perfectly. Happiness had been a long time coming for Nessa, but since she'd met Miles Trevellion just over three months ago her life had changed for the better.

Sheena tried not to sigh at the romance that had blossomed between her two friends, wishing it was her instead. She'd given up her one chance at *true* love ten years ago and it was a mistake she'd have to live with for the rest of her life.

'Thanks for everything,' Janessa said, her words filled with meaning. 'You're the best sister a girl ever had.'

Sheena felt tears start to well in her eyes and quickly blinked them away. 'I'd do anything for you,' she replied, hugging Janessa carefully, emotion rising within her.

'All right, you two,' Kaycee said. 'No tears or we'll be another fifteen minutes fixing our make-up and I doubt Miles will be able to contain his impatience.'

'True. True,' Sheena remarked as Kaycee handed her a bouquet of white roses. The two bridesmaids wore long, ruby-red dresses with sexy slits up the sides. Janessa accepted her bridal bouquet of ruby-red roses and held them in front of her with slightly trembling hands.

'Stunning.' Sheena nodded in approval before the photographer came in to take one last photograph of the three women together.

'Time to head down the aisle,' Kaycee said, and, squaring her shoulders, walked out of the little room, leaving Janessa and Sheena together for a brief moment, the music from the quartet surrounding them.

'I'm so happy for you, Nessa. Really. No one deserves this more than you.'

Janessa blew Sheena a kiss.

'Ready?' Sheena stepped out the door, ensuring the train of Janessa's dress didn't get tangled. They walked on the red carpet laid out in the hangar, which had been decorated with a mixture of roses and wild flowers. Garlands hung around the hangar and also on Janessa's beloved Tiger Moth biplane, which was just outside the door.

Everyone stood as Kaycee started to walk

down the aisle, between the rows of chairs which had been set out for the guests. Sheena smiled once more at her friend then turned to look towards the groom standing at the other end of the aisle.

Miles was waiting impatiently for his bride. Beside Miles stood his father, acting as best man as Miles's first choice for best man—Will Beckman—was still in America and had been unable to make it back for the wedding.

Sheena was relieved at that. She and Will had history and a shared romantic past that hadn't ended happily. Sheena turned back and gave Janessa one more smile before holding her bouquet in front of her, shoulders back, head held high. Time to walk slowly but surely down the aisle. She lifted her foot, took one step, glanced up to where Miles was waiting…and faltered.

Will!

He was standing there. Between Miles and his father. Will was here. *Will was here!*

She blinked her eyes once…twice…as though trying to clear her vision, trying to tell herself that she'd imagined him standing there, looking so devastatingly handsome in a tuxedo, a red boutonniere pinned to his lapel, his hair slightly ruffled by the cool July breeze outside.

She blinked again. It was definitely him. Will was now standing beside Miles, the two men sharing a quick but firm handshake and pat on the back. He'd made it just in time for his best friend's wedding.

Sheena's mouth went instantly dry, her heart starting to pound wildly in her chest, the noise thrumming through her body, almost deafening her. She gripped her bouquet tighter, channelling all the panic and fear, which seemed to have hit her like a tidal wave, into the stems of the flowers.

How could he be here? Miles had told her only yesterday that Will was unable to make the wedding because he'd been delayed by a sick patient. Until then, Sheena had been psyching herself up to see Will again. She'd gone over polite little sentences in her head in order to make small talk with him. She'd pondered whether he'd changed much during the past decade. She'd stressed over his reception of her—would it be friendly or antagonistic? She'd lost sleep over the prospect of seeing him again so when Miles had told her Will wouldn't be able to make it, she had been intensely relieved.

And now he was here! He'd made it. She had no idea how or why but… She blinked again, clearing her vision, registering the scene before her. Nervous anxiety exploded within every cell of her body, her stomach flipping and turning. She gripped the flowers even tighter, trying in vain to steel herself. She would have to speak to him now, smile politely, be cool and calm, yet she felt anything but. It was necessary to have contact with him, given that he was the best man and she was the maid of honour, but for all the different scenarios she'd worked through in her mind, she now found she couldn't remember a thing.

Will was here. At the end of the aisle. Standing next to Miles, his tuxedo making him appear crisp, debonair and excessively sexy. Her heart skipped a beat and she tried not to remember what it had been like to kiss him.

Will was in the same room as her—breathing

the same air—for the first time in ten years. It couldn't be…but it was. He had come and now *she* had to face him.

Sheena swallowed convulsively, her gaze trained solely on the man who had once meant the world to her. Will Beckman. They'd been so in love…and then it had ended. *She* had ended it and Will had hated her for it.

'Sheena?' Janessa's concerned tone from behind snapped Sheena back to the present. 'Something wrong?'

Sheena turned and looked at Janessa. 'Will is *here.*'

'Oh, great.' Janessa beamed. 'He made it. Miles will be so happy. Go. Go, Sheenie. That's your cue.' Janessa urged her friend forward and there was nothing else for Sheena to do except to turn, paste on a smile and walk down the aisle.

Because of the shock she'd just received, it was a wonder she could actually remember how to walk, let alone do it in time to the music. Will was here. The thought played over and over in her mind, as though stuck, and each step she took brought her closer towards him.

The aisle seemed to stretch on for ever and if she'd had half the chance, she would have turned tail and bolted as far away as possible…but she could never do that to Janessa. Sheena kept her eyes trained straight ahead, smile fixed firmly in place, one slow step at a time.

All too soon, she was standing opposite him, everyone turning to see the bride walk down the aisle—Sheena and Will on opposite sides of the makeshift altar. She knew she should be watching Janessa but she couldn't resist a quick glance his way…and was startled to find him looking at *her*.

Quickly averting her gaze, her heart started pounding even faster against her ribs and she glued her eyes to her friend, unable to believe he'd caught her sneaking a glance at him. She had no idea how her legs were still holding her up as her entire body was shaking with adrenaline at being so close to him. Good heavens, he was handsome but, then, he always had been. So handsome. So tall. So…Will.

Her breathing had now almost reached the point of hyperventilation. She parted her lips to allow the pent-up air to escape, wondering what sort of reception she would receive from him. She wouldn't blame him at all if he didn't speak a word to her but she hoped, more for Miles's and Janessa's sakes, that that wasn't the case.

Janessa finished her walk down the aisle and Sheena accepted the bridal bouquet, glad to have something to do. She watched as her two friends held hands—eager to be married, love, honour and devotion shining clearly from their faces.

Throughout the nuptials, Sheena risked quite a number of glances at Will, her mind still processing the fact that he was standing not six feet away from her. Was he still angry about the way things had ended between them? Had he managed to forgive her sometime during the past decade? Had he moved on with his life? Found someone to spend his time with? She quickly checked his hands but found them ringless. Still, that didn't mean he wasn't attached. It didn't matter to her whether or not he had someone— all she'd ever wanted for Will was his happiness.

'I now pronounce you husband and wife,' the minister announced, and Sheena jolted her thoughts back to the present, unable to believe the ceremony was done and dusted. Had she been in la-la land the whole time? 'You may now kiss your bride.'

Miles leaned forward and lifted the veil from Janessa's face before sliding his arms around his new wife's waist and drawing their bodies into close contact. Sheena couldn't help but smile at his antics, knowing Miles was determined to kiss his new wife thoroughly.

She was incredibly happy for both her friends and, with a bright smile still on her lips, she glanced over at Will, astonished to find him once more looking back at her. Sheena's heart skipped a beat and she couldn't help but gasp, her eyes widening in surprise. She knew she should probably look away, pay attention to her friends, but she couldn't. She was like a deer caught in the headlights, his blue eyes as rich and deep and compelling as they'd always been.

His gaze flicked from her eyes down to her lips before quickly scanning her body in a visual caress that filled her with heat and flooded her body with a longing she'd long since forgotten.

Did he still like what he saw? She hoped she looked good, especially considering that three months ago she'd given birth to twin girls... and not just *any* twins but conjoined twins. Her figure, she knew, was more curvy than it had been ten years ago. Did he still find her attractive? And why did it matter so much to her?

Janessa once more brought Sheena's thoughts back to the present as she reached around for her bouquet. Sheena snapped her eyes away from the alluring Will Beckman and realised that she'd missed the inaugural kiss and that everyone in the hangar was now clapping and cheering the newlyweds.

The bride and groom started back down the aisle, stopping to receive warm wishes from their friends and family. Sheena stepped forward, as did Will. He was the best man. She was the maid of honour. Kaycee, the other bridesmaid, would be partnered by Miles's father, who was the other groomsman. Sheena took another step closer to Will and breathed in a strong, calming breath...or at least that was what she'd planned to do. Instead, she breathed in the earthy, fresh scent she'd always equated with him and tried not to sigh with longing.

With another step he stood beside her, crooking his elbow in her direction, ready to escort her down the aisle behind the happy couple.

'Hello, Dr Woodcombe.' His tone was brisk, crisp and efficient, as though he were simply saying good morning to a member of staff at a ward round. Sheena slipped her hand around his elbow, heat suffusing through her at the touch. She tried not to be concerned with his impersonal greeting. They had been a couple a long time ago but surely the fact that they *had* been together afforded her something more than a perfunctory greeting. She licked her dry lips, belatedly remembering she was wearing far more make-up than she was used to and it wouldn't do to have all her lipstick disappear before they started posing for photographs.

'Hello, Will.' She tried to ensure her own voice was without emotion. She tried to clear her throat but there was nothing there for her to clear. She continued to keep her pasted smile in place as guests snapped pictures of the wedding party. 'I see you managed to make it in time. Well done.'

He glanced briefly down at her as they took another few steps and stopped as both Janessa and Miles paused to hug and greet more well-wishers. 'No doubt you probably wished I hadn't made it at all.'

She was stunned that his comment was so spot on. 'What makes you say that?'

'I saw the look of shock on your face before you started to walk down the aisle.'

She closed her eyes for a brief moment. Oh. Had he? How embarrassing…how telling. His comment made her feel naked, stripped bare as though after all these years he was still able to see right through her, that he still had some sort of power over her. She hated feeling so exposed. 'Miles wanted you here. That's all that matters.'

They took another step forward, another camera flash lighting the air around them, both of them smiling politely.

'I understand congratulations are in order,' he said after a moment, his words clipped.

'For?'

'Did you not give birth to two little girls?'

'Oh. Yes.' At the mention of her daughters, Sheena's smile became natural, her eyes sparkling with happiness, yet at the same time she felt highly self-conscious discussing her daughters with Will. The main reason she'd turned down his proposal all those years ago had been because she'd been unable to have children, and now she had *two*.

'I'm sorry, Sheena,' her specialist had said when she'd been about eighteen years old. 'The chances of you ever having children are extremely slim. Your endometriosis is too severe.'

When Will had repeatedly talked of his plans for a large family and how much having children meant to him, she'd known she would never end up spending her life with him, even though back then she'd loved him dearly.

Now, though, she had Ellie and Sarah. Her babies, her girls, and they were her two incredible miracles she'd been assured by the finest specialists would never happen.

'How are they coping?' he continued when she didn't elaborate. 'Of course I've received status updates from Miles but it would be good to have the mother's opinion of the situation, especially as she's a trained paediatrician.'

'As a paediatrician, I have to say they're doing incredibly well. As a mother...' She paused for a moment and smiled. 'I have to say that they are the most beautiful, wonderful little girls on the face of this earth.'

Will clenched his jaw at her words, annoyed with himself for being affected by the sweet smile on her face. She hadn't changed much in the ten years since they'd parted. Her hair was shorter and she looked tired around the eyes, even beneath the make-up.

Sheena. A mother. The woman who had told him she couldn't marry him because she could never give him children. Well, she'd been able to give some other man children so perhaps there had been other reasons why she hadn't wanted to be with him but hadn't been courageous or honest enough to admit them. Never again would he allow himself to succumb to her. Once bitten, twice shy and all that. She'd had her chance and she'd rejected him. He'd moved on and he congratulated himself for being professional and polite towards Sheena.

They took another step down the aisle and stopped as more people greeted the bride and groom in front of them.

'Hang on, what did you think I was congratulating you for?' he asked a moment later.

'Uh…nothing.' She shook her head.

'You may as well tell me everything because we're going to be stuck halfway down this aisle for another few minutes. Besides, if you've achieved more milestones in your life, how am I to congratulate you if I don't know about them?' Although his words seemed polite, she could hear slight curiosity in his tone. Was he as curious about her as she was about him?

'It's no big deal.' She shrugged a shoulder. 'It's just I signed my divorce papers last week.' She went to take another step forward but found that Will had stopped. She looked up at him.

'You're not married?' There was a hint of incredulity in his tone.

'That's generally what the word *divorced* means, Will,' she countered.

'And you thought I was offering congratulations on that?'

'You did mention that Miles had been giving you updates.'

'On the *girls*, not your private life.'

Sheena shrugged, knowing that even if Miles had let something slip about Sheena's present life, it would never have been done with malicious intent. Janessa and Miles both wanted Sheena to be happy with someone new, but she was the mother of twins and her girls had to be her main focus from now on. The chances of she and Will reuniting as a couple wasn't on the cards either. A decade was a long time and both of them had clearly changed.

'In a way, my divorce is sort of worth celebrating.'

'How so?'

'I'm ending a part of my life which, ever since I was told I was pregnant, has given me nothing but grief. Now, at least, I can focus solely on the girls.' There was complete commitment and determination in her tone. 'I'm going to be the best mother I can possibly be.'

'You always were full of determination.' Will glanced down at her and she was surprised to see a small half-smile teasing his mouth. 'Some might say stubborn—'

'Hey!' she interrupted, but found her own lips twitching into a smile.

'But we'll stick with determined for now.'

'Thank you.' Sheena was secretly pleased that after a few minutes in each other's company, Will had felt comfortable enough to tease her a little. Was it possible they could form a relationship that was more than just professional? A loose friendship perhaps?

Even when they'd been dating, they'd always been good friends and right now, given that she wasn't looking for any sort of permanent relationship with any man, she needed as many friends as she could get.

Of course, there was no doubting Will's appeal. The man was still the most handsome man she'd ever seen and with the way she was still tingling with excitement at being so close to him, it was clear he still maintained that unassuming sensuality she'd first been attracted to all those years ago.

They managed to take another few steps down the aisle, drawing closer to the end. The heat from his body, the scent of whatever aftershave he was wearing, so earthy, so spicy, settled around her, enticing her to remember just how close they'd been in the past. Soon she would be able to let go of Will's arm and at least put a bit of breathing room between them before they had to pose for more photographs. When they finally reached the end of the aisle, Sheena quickly slipped her hand from his arm.

'Excuse me. I'll be right back,' she murmured, before slipping away from where the photographer and everyone else was busy snapping photographs of the bride and groom. She knew as maid of honour she should be there, that she should stay by Janessa's side, helping her with whatever she needed, but…well, Janessa had Miles now and Sheena needed some air.

Heading around the outside of the hangar, the heels of her shoes sinking into the grass, she walked to the small bathroom and ran her hands beneath the cool water for a moment. She wanted to splash water onto her face, to shock her thoughts back to reality, but she couldn't even do that because of the make-up she was wearing.

High heels, dresses, make-up, fancy hair-styles—they just weren't her, and right at that moment, even though she loved Janessa and Miles very dearly, all she wanted was to be back at the hospital with her little girls. Kissing them, talking to them, feeding them, loving them. She closed her eyes, missing them so badly it was starting to hurt.

Seeing Will again had rocked her neat and or-dered little world from its axis. Her comfortable life had been turned upside down and inside out at the first sight of him.

The fact that he still looked incredible didn't help at all. Where she'd thought she'd be able to put what had happened between them into the past, to look forward to her new life with her girls—even though she knew the next nine months weren't going to be an easy road—her anxieties had hit the roof the instant she'd seen him standing at the other end of that aisle next to Miles.

Will Beckman. She closed her eyes, remembering how incredible it had felt being held by him, being close to him, laughing with him, kissing him. She sighed, breathing out her memories with soft longing. However, that was all in the past.

'Sheena?' Kaycee called. 'Are you in there, honey?' A second later, Kaycee walked into the small room. 'Oh, there you are. The photographer needs us.'

Sheena turned, putting on a smile for her friend, knowing she would not let Janessa down even though she felt like hiding in the bathroom for the rest of the day. 'Ready when you are.'

They headed back out to where Janessa and Miles were posing against *Ruby*, Janessa's beloved biplane that her father had lovingly restored and named after her mother.

'They look so happy,' she murmured.

'Yes. They do,' a deep voice replied from just behind her, and she turned, a little startled as she'd been expecting Kaycee to answer. 'Are you all right, Sheena?'

'I'm fine.' She swallowed over the obvious lie. Being near Will, standing close to him, talking to him, made her feel anything but fine. He was the reason she was in a dither but there was no way she was going to confess that to him.

Kaycee headed off to find Miles's father so that the entire bridal party could be reassembled for more photographs. Will leaned in closer, his breath fanning Sheena's neck as he spoke. 'Liar,' he whispered softly, before easing away.

'What do you know about it?' she asked as they both headed over to where Miles was helping Janessa up onto the wing of the plane, ensuring her wedding dress and veil didn't tear. The heels of Sheena's shoes once more sank into the grass as she walked and she realised she must look highly undignified…but at the moment she really didn't care.

Will stopped walking and looked at her. 'I know you, Sheena. I know you better than I know myself sometimes and I know when you're lying.'

She scoffed at that but knew he spoke the truth. He *did* know her, just as she knew him equally well. 'Fine. Then I'm not all right. OK?'

'Because of me?'

'Yes, because of you. I…hadn't expected to see you today. Janessa said last night that you weren't able to make it.'

'I was only able to make it because the patient I've been caring for stabilised early this morning, giving me a short window in which to fly from Melbourne to Adelaide and attend the ceremony. At this stage I'm not quite sure how long I'll be staying as we're due to be flying back to the States later this evening.'

'Transferring a patient from Melbourne to Philadelphia?' When Miles had told her Will wouldn't be able to make it because he was transferring a patient, Sheena had assumed Will was still in the States, not already here in Australia.

'Yes. Two-year-old boy with early signs of rheumatoid arthritis. Some vascular colleagues have developed a new way of assisting young children with this disease and have asked me to consult in an orthopaedic capacity, hence why I've flown to Australia to escort the patient and his family to the States.'

'That sounds like incredible research, Will.' She could talk about medicine with him, especially as it meant the conversation wasn't focused on her. 'You were always so good with sick children. You have a knack of making them feel relaxed and cared for.'

Will paused for a moment then cleared his throat. 'Thank you, Sheena.' Her words had surprised him. He'd been prepared to see Sheena again, prepared to keep his distance, to treat her merely as the mother of the conjoined twins he would one day help separate. What he hadn't banked on were the effects of her smiles and sincere words. He'd also expected her to be married and the news that she was recently divorced had thrown him. He shook his head. It didn't matter if she was single, it didn't matter if she looked as incredible now as she had ten years ago. She was still the woman who had turned down his marriage proposal and then years later married another man and had had children—

children she'd told him she would *never* be able to conceive.

'You're a brilliant doctor, Will, and I know your work can be rather intense,' Sheena continued. 'Being an orthopaedic paediatrician who specialises primarily in neonatology carries with it a heavy workload. Miles has often talked of the work you've done together and now other specialities are appreciating your gift.' She looked up at him. 'Does the work you do make you happy?'

He frowned at the question, finding it a little odd. 'Of course it does. I wouldn't do it if it didn't challenge me or make me happy.'

'Good.' She nodded. 'I'd hate you to be hiding yourself away in your work.'

'What's that supposed to mean? That because you turned my marriage proposal down a decade ago, I'd be so lost without you I would throw myself into my work and forget about living?'

Mortification crossed Sheena's face. 'No. I merely meant that as a vibrant, handsome man it would be a great shame if you focused solely on work.' He continued to glare at her and she started to feel a little uncomfortable. 'Despite what you might think, Will, I've only ever wanted you to be happy, to be able to fulfil your dreams.'

He caught a glimpse of Kaycee, the other bridesmaid, heading in their direction, with Miles's father in tow.

Will eased a little closer to Sheena, his voice low, his eyes sharp and piercing. Sheena tried not to gasp at the darkness around him. 'Are you saying that you turned my proposal down because you didn't want to destroy my dreams?'

She'd never seen him look like that before—ever. This was a new expression, a different side to Will, and in that one moment she realised that perhaps she didn't know him as well as she'd previously thought.

'Yes.' The word was barely a whisper and she tried to step back, to put a bit of distance be-tween them, but the heels of her shoes had sunk into the grass.

'And what about the other man you married?' Will continued. 'Did you care about his dreams?'

Sheena winced a little at Will's words. Did he

think her devoid of all emotion? Pain pierced her heart to think he thought ill of her. 'Of course I did.' She frowned as she answered, conscious of keeping her voice down so they didn't disturb Janessa and Miles. She was aware that at any moment they'd be called on to stand side by side and smile brightly for the camera but first there was something she needed to say.

'You know nothing about my life, Will. A lot can happen to a person in ten years and that's exactly what has happened to me—a lot. My relationship with Jonas is none of your business, just as your own relationships over the past decade have nothing to do with me. We were a couple. We broke up. We moved on.'

'Agreed, but—' he leaned even closer, his blue eyes flashing with dangerous excitement '—aren't you the least bit curious?' His gaze dipped to encompass her parted lips, unable to believe the way he'd felt watching her eyes light up with emotion. He'd always been attracted to her, even more so when she'd been angry. He breathed in, tantalised by the strawberry scent he'd always equated with her. He looked at her eyes again, admiring the way they'd widened in surprise at his nearness.

It was clear he could still affect her and he tried not to preen a little at that realisation. 'Curious about me?' His tone was deep, rich, sensual, yet with a hint of menace, drawing her in, hypnotising her. 'I'm definitely curious about you. I want to know what you've been doing. Why you finally married and had children, especially when you told me you couldn't.'

Her gaze was fixed on his mouth, her heart pounding as she watched his lips form the words. 'I find myself wanting answers to the questions that have been buried in the back of my mind for so very long…and given I'll soon be in Australia, caring for your daughters, seeing you every day, I intend to get them.'

CHAPTER TWO

SHEENA paced back and forth in front of the crib that held her two very special little girls. Her agitation level was high, her anxiety was through the roof, and for some reason she seemed unable to stop wringing her hands.

Ellie and Sarah, her two beautiful babies, were sleeping peacefully in their specially designed crib, the girls conjoined at the hip. Sarah had her thumb in her mouth and Ellie sucked on a pacifier. They may be conjoined but the six-month-old twins most certainly had their different personalities. Sarah, so gung-ho, letting everyone know she was around, whilst Ellie was placid and patient.

The pacing, however, didn't cease. Back and forth Sheena went. Wringing her hands, heart pounding wildly. The girls had been moved one month ago from the neonate intensive care unit to a private room in the paediatric wing. They were still garnering a lot of media attention, especially with the date of their impending separation drawing closer every day.

'You can do this. You can do this,' Sheena said over and over, wiping her hands down her pale pink skirt. She fidgeted with her cream-coloured shirt and checked her short black hair in the mirror, her blue eyes wide with fear. Anyone watching her might think she was nervous and apprehensive because in a few days' time her daughters would be undergoing one of the biggest and intricate surgical procedures of the medical profession…but that wasn't the case.

'You can do this. You can do this,' she repeated, giving her hands a shake before starting to wring them once more.

Her girls had already had several smaller operations to insert tissue expanders, helping them to grow extra skin so that when the separation was complete, there would be skin to cover the open wounds around their hips. They'd also had many anaesthetics, especially when having CT scans. This was so the neonate team could quite clearly see what veins and arteries the two girls shared. As a paediatrician herself, Sheena was well aware of all the negatives and positives surrounding these procedures and whilst she'd been anxious and concerned for her girls each and every time they were wheeled away, it was nothing compared to the complete and encompassing agitation she was feeling now and it was all because of Will.

Seeing him at the wedding had been nerve-racking enough, without him saying that he was curious about her. When he'd leaned forward, looked at her so intently with those big blue eyes of his and a look that could still weaken her knees, she'd known she was in trouble. She knew she'd hurt Will all those years ago when she'd rejected his proposal, but she'd had to. Loving him the way she had, she'd chosen to make the sacrifice of breaking it off while there had still been a chance for both of them to find some sort of happiness with someone else.

He had desperately wanted children. She hadn't been able to give them to him. In her mind, it had been as clear as that. She'd rather he hated her for rejecting his proposal, for breaking their relationship, than agreeing to marry him and then having him reject her when he discovered he could never have that family he'd always dreamed about.

Hearing him say he was curious about her, about the decisions she'd made in her life since they'd parted, had caused a mass of tingles to wash over her in anxious anticipation. He'd been so close, his breath fanning her cheek, his lips moving almost in slow motion as his rich, earthy scent, tinged with hypnotic spices, had wound its way around her, causing her to almost hyperventilate.

A second later, Kaycee had marshalled them all into position for the next group photograph, Sheena powerfully aware of every slight move Will had made. When the photographer had asked Will to place his hand around Sheena's waist, her body had become a riot of suppressed excitement at being so close to Will once again. His hand hadn't been shy or tentative but instead he'd drawn her close, as though it had been the most natural thing in the world. As they'd smiled for the camera, she'd felt the heat radiating out from his body, felt his veiled determination in the quest he'd just started and could feel the high level of awareness they'd both felt at being so close to one another again.

When they'd shifted positions, this time standing behind the bride and groom, almost facing each other, her hand on Will's shoulder, his hand resting in the small of her back, Sheena had found it not only mentally distracting to be so close to him but increasingly difficult to keep her smile in place as Will had been moving his thumb in slow, small circles, driving her to distraction.

'Stop,' she whispered between her polite smiles.

'Why? I know you like it.'

'Will!'

'I can't help it if I have intimate knowledge about you, Sheena.'

'So you're going to deliberately use it against me? To drive me wild with annoyance?' The photograph was taken and they were told they could move. Will, however, held her for a second longer.

'No. To drive you wild with *longing*.' His deep, dark voice had washed over her and even when he'd released her from his hold, she wasn't able to move for a whole thirty seconds. His eyes told her he was determined to follow through on his quest to extract from her the answers he required.

Then, before she'd had a chance to suss him out further, before she'd been able to get a firm hold on exactly what he wanted to know, Will was forced to leave the wedding before the reception even started because his patient in Melbourne required his immediate attention.

Sheena had been left with a sense of impending doom hanging over her head for the past three months. Every now and then she would wake from her sleep, gasping with that wild longing he'd promised her she'd feel. How was it that after so many years he still had the ability to affect her?

'Breathe. Breathe,' she whispered again, trying

to listen to that small, still voice in her mind that was desperate to calm her down.

'Hey, Sheenie.'

Sheena jumped and whirled round, her eyes becoming even wider as someone entered the room. A split second later she relaxed and breathed a sigh of relief as Janessa walked towards her.

'Oh, Nessa. You scared me.' She pressed her hands to her chest.

Janessa hugged her friend, the two women as close as sisters. 'What's wrong? Is it the girls?' Janessa immediately looked across at the twins, lying in their specially designed crib. As one of the neonatologists assigned to the twins, Janessa was completely in love with both her goddaughters, and was providing the best care possible for them.

Janessa's husband, Miles Trevellion, was the neonate surgeon in charge of the entire team of specialists responsible for the upcoming separation of the twins. During the past six months, Miles and Janessa had been Sheena's stabilising support but now Sheena wasn't at all sure they'd be able to do anything about the impending doom that awaited her.

'The girls are fine. Perfect. Beautiful. Fine.'

Janessa looked closely at Sheena. 'You're pacing. You're wringing your hands. You're… highly agitated.' She continued to watch her friend, thinking quickly. 'In fact…I haven't seen you this agitated since my wedding.'

Sheena stopped pacing and flung her arms out wide. 'There's only one man in the world who can bring me to this level of agitation!'

'Will.' Janessa nodded. 'Do you know, when you spotted him at the other end of the aisle, I had the briefest thought that you might turn tail and run.' She smiled warmly at her friend, her words carrying no malice.

Sheena laughed without humour, the sound holding a tinge of repressed hysteria. 'I was highly tempted but I wasn't going to ruin your big day.'

'And I thank you for that. What I don't quite understand—' Janessa sat down in one of the comfortable chairs '—is that you've known for months that Will would be treating the girls. Besides, you both seemed OK at the wedding.'

'That's only because neither of us wanted to make a big fuss on your special day but now he's not here for a few hours, he's not here to pose and smile for the camera. He's here for at least the next two months and I'll no doubt be seeing him almost every single day of those two months.'

'Are you worried that the old spark might rekindle?' Janessa waggled her eyebrows up and down for emphasis.

Sheena closed her eyes, not ready to admit that the 'old spark', as Janessa termed it, had been reignited at the wedding...or at least something had been awakened. Seeing that determined look in Will's eyes had made him seem ruthless, dangerous, tempting...and that had excited her.

She sighed with confusion and looked at her friend, starting to pace again. 'I don't know,' she told Janessa. 'I'm the type of person who likes to understand her parameters so I can work within them. I've had to make some very difficult decisions throughout my life, I've had to endure a lot of unfun things, but the whole time I at least knew where I'd come from and where I was going.' She shook her head. 'That doesn't happen with Will. He twists me up inside and turns my otherwise intelligent mind to mush with just one of his gorgeous, deep, smouldering looks.' Sheena stopped pacing, her hands now clutched against her chest.

'Wow. This guy really does wind you up, doesn't he?' Janessa stated rhetorically.

'Arrgh. What am I supposed to do?' Sheena covered her face with her hands then indicated the door. 'He's coming here *today*, Nessa. He'll be here soon. Will! Will is coming here. To see me and the g—' She stopped talking, suddenly finding it difficult to breathe as the impact of her situation seemed to hit with full force. She felt hot and cold and fanned her face with her hands as she tried to calm her breathing. She didn't resist when Janessa forced her to sit.

'You've gone as white as a ghost. I had no idea that Will sent you into such a tizz. Quick, put your head between your knees before you faint.'

Janessa urged Sheena's head down. 'Now stay there while I go and get a paper bag.'

Sheena closed her eyes, doing as she was told. Why was it that the mere thought of seeing Will again could affect her in this manner? Was it because he was determined to find answers? Would she be able to give him answers that would satisfy him? They'd met in England while both working on their registrar rotations. They'd become friends then started to date. They'd become serious, more deeply involved than Sheena had thought possible.

Then her rotation had come to an end and the week before she'd been due to return to Australia Will had proposed. Seeing the devastation on his face, the shock, the disbelief when she'd told him she could never have children, that it was a medical impossibility, had broken her heart but confirmed the truth of why she'd needed to turn him down. There was no way she could give him the happiness he deserved. Sheena had finished the last week of her rotation, avoiding Will wherever possible, and had then returned to Australia, to her life without him.

Now Will was one of the world's leading orthopaedic paediatric specialists for conjoined twins. He was coming here to care for the daughters she'd been told she would never have.

Her *miracle* babies.

The door to the room opened. 'Quick. Give me that bag,' Sheena urged, and, with head still down between her knees, she held out her hand.

'Hello, Sheena.' The deep, rich, unforgettable tones of William Beckman filled the room and Sheena froze for a second before dropping her arm, lifting her head and standing up. The sudden action, especially as she'd had her head down, made her feel dizzy and she stumbled.

'Whoa. Easy.' He was by her side in a flash, his firm, muscled arms slipping about her waist as he drew her close, steadying her against him. 'No need to get up on my account.' The vibrations from his voice rumbled through her as she placed a hand weakly against his chest, memories of the last time he'd held her like this, been this close to her, within kissing distance, flooding through her mind as she slowly raised her gaze to mesh with his.

Blue eyes met blue eyes and she sighed, transported back to the day they'd spent together at Brighton. Two Aussies, out to find a bit of sun during a typical English summer. Having a few days off from the hospital, they'd headed off to Brighton, standing on the pebbly beach, their arms about each other as they'd watched the sun disappear and the stars start to twinkle above them.

They'd both been so happy.

Sheena sighed, allowing herself this one brief moment of reflection, her gaze still locked with his. How was it possible that after all this time she was still so affected by his nearness? As she continued to stare into his eyes, she saw that hint of darkness, that strong, powerful difference she'd witnessed at the wedding. He quirked an eyebrow at her.

'Feeling better?' The words were rich and deep and resonated throughout her entire body.

Sheena stared at his lips, hoping her mind was capable of understanding what he'd just said. It was clear that she was uncomfortable but with the way he'd just caught her sitting, it brought instantly to mind the very first time they'd met. Sheena had been lying on the floor, trying to get a tiny toy car out from beneath a heavy cupboard in the paediatric playroom. She'd located the toy car, stood and then thrust the car high into the air in triumph.

The children around her had clapped, impressed with her rescue skills, and it hadn't been until one of the children had pointed out that another doctor had entered the playroom that Sheena had even known he'd been there all along, watching her every move—*and* she'd been wearing a skirt. After they'd been dating a while, he'd confessed to her that it had been the sexiest toy rescue he'd ever witnessed.

She'd handed the car back to the child, all the time staring at Will in a way that had made him incredibly aware of the instant tension buzzing between them. When he'd held out his hand to introduce himself, she'd stood there for several seconds before shaking it.

'Sheena?' he prompted, trying not to breathe in her sweet, strawberry scent.

'Uh… Um…' As though only just realising

she was still in his arms, she instantly shifted, moving away, putting some distance between them. 'Yeah… I'm… I'm fine. Thanks.' She waved her hands in the air, as though she was trying to make the past minute or two disappear. 'And you? How are you since I saw you last?' Her gaze flicked over him in a quick but thorough appraisal and she swallowed, unable to believe he looked better than he had at the wedding.

'Fine.'

Had his lips just twitched when he'd said that? She thought she'd detected a slight twitch. Was he amused by her silly antics? With the fact that she'd been head down, tail up when he'd first walked into the room, before becoming dizzy?

She watched as he put his hands into his pockets and with that one move it was as though he'd switched on his professional persona. *Dr* Will Beckman was now in the room. 'I trust the past three months have been good for you and your girls?'

'Yes. Yes, they have.' She nodded for extra emphasis, a little intrigued with his politeness and the way he seemed intent on keeping his distance. From the way he'd left things at the wedding, saying he was curious about her, she'd half expected him to waltz in here and pin her with twenty questions. 'They've both responded well to the surgeries.'

'I'm pleased to hear that.'

'Oh, by the way, how's your patient with rheumatoid arthritis? The one you flew to Australia to collect back in July?'

Both of Will's eyebrows rose in surprise, revealing a glimpse of the Will she'd known in the past. It was sort of strange to be around him, familiar with his facial expressions and mannerisms and yet not really knowing the man he'd become during the past decade. She was seeing two sides to him and realised the brisk, direct man, the one who seemed to harness a hint of darkness about him, the one who'd both startled and excited her at the wedding, was the one she knew she needed to be wary of.

'Doing well. Thankfully he responded extremely well to the new treatment and was able to return to Australia about a fortnight ago.' He nodded, pleased with the satisfactory outcome of that situation.

'That's wonderful news. I've often thought about you…er…about you and him and his… you know…his case and the research and treatment and…everything. I'm glad it all worked out.'

Will gave her a curious look. 'I'm astonished that with everything you've had going on with your girls you would have even given him another thought. Then again, you always were a considerate doctor, especially when children were involved.' His words were spoken softly, tenderly and then, almost as though he'd caught himself praising her, he quickly straightened his shoulders and clenched his jaw, his expression changing from one of open appreciation to an unreadable mask. He crossed his arms over his chest and inclined his head towards the crib.

'Aren't you going to introduce me to your daughters?' His tone was professional once again.

'Oh. Right. Of course. How silly of me.' Sheena shook her head as she walked over to the crib where the girls lay, unable to believe she'd momentarily forgotten they were even in the room. Ellie was lying there, eyes open, content simply to look around the room. Sarah, thankfully, was sleeping. 'Hello, baby,' Sheena crooned as she stroked Ellie's cheek. Ellie's little eyelids fluttered closed for a moment before she looked at her mother. 'I didn't know you were awake.' Sheena leaned over and brushed a soft kiss over Ellie's forehead.

'Ellie, this is Will. Will, this is Ellie. Sarah, the rowdy one of the two, is thankfully sleeping.'

'Rowdy, eh?' There was a slight thickness to his tone as he watched her with the babies. She looked so right, so complete standing there, touching their soft skin, kissing them.

'They may be conjoined but they have very different personalities. It's as though they really are two halves of the same whole.'

He nodded, desperate not to be affected with the way she looked near the babies. So calm and happy and…right. He clenched his jaw, hardening his heart against the sight before him. He'd come here to treat the girls, to be a part of the team that would separate them and give them the best chance at living normal, healthy lives. Nothing more. The fact that he wanted answers from Sheena was a bonus and perhaps once she provided him with the truth about why she'd rejected his proposal ten years ago, he'd finally achieve closure on that chapter in his life. He was certain that she'd lied to him, that she'd used the possibility of infertility as an excuse. The evidence of that lie was before him right now. Two babies—*Sheena's* babies.

He nodded. 'That's the way it is with the majority of conjoined twins. One rowdy, one quiet. It's also the way it is with twins in general, especially identical ones.'

'Miles says the same thing.'

'I guess, as we've both been working in the field of separating conjoined twins for quite some time now, that we share similar views and opinions on the subject.'

'You're the experts. All I know is that Sarah is the one who screams the loudest, who eats the most and who demands all the attention. Ellie, however, doesn't seem to be at all jealous of her sister's vivacity. Ellie's very quiet, very content. Some days I worry about her more.' There was a wistfulness to Sheena's tone and she brushed another kiss across Ellie's forehead. 'My quiet achiever. See how, even though she's awake, she doesn't move or wriggle or make too much noise?'

Will nodded. 'She doesn't want to wake Sarah. She's smart. Sarah may have the sass but Ellie definitely knows what's what.'

Sheena laughed. 'I guess you're right. I've never thought of it that way.'

And he'd never thought he'd hear that sweet, relaxed laugh of hers ever again. When she'd left England to return to Australia at the end of her rotation, his world had been devastated. Since then, he'd only been back in to Australia for brief visits to see his parents and siblings, and each time he'd made sure there had been no way he would ever run into Sheena—the woman who had broken his heart into tiny pieces. This time, though, there had been no avoiding the issue. First they'd been thrown together at Miles and

Janessa's wedding and now they'd be seeing each other almost daily because of her daughters.

Now here he stood, back in Australia, back with Sheena, looking down at *her* children in the crib. The little girls were gorgeous and definitely had their mother's colouring in their bright blue eyes and dark hair. So incredibly beautiful.

He'd always wanted a big family. Little girls and little boys, and he'd wanted them with Sheena. The perfect family. Having been raised in a large, loving home himself, he'd carried this ideal picture with him, only to find that life never turned out the way you planned.

'How is it that you can know so much about the girls when you've only just walked into the room?' Sheena glanced up at him, amazed at his skill. 'You were always so good at diagnosing patients, having a bond with them after only a few minutes in their presence. I always envied you that ability.'

When he looked at her, he was astonished to find her blue eyes filled with wonderment and appreciation. He swallowed over the sudden dryness in his throat. Flashes of the times they'd spent together, the way they'd laughed, the way they'd shared intimate moments, the way she'd broken his heart… The images flicked through his mind, one after the other, before he closed the mental door in his mind and hardened his heart.

'I've been working with conjoined twins for quite some time now, Sheena. Recognising their individuality is one of the first aspects of effective care and one that most professionals in this field acquire quite quickly.'

Sheena placed one last kiss on Ellie's forehead before straightening. She hadn't missed the way his blue eyes had turned from calm and collected to dark and stormy. She knew him so well that at times it was easy for her to read his expressions. It shouldn't be that way. Not after all these years.

The fact that their paths had crossed again, under the most far-fetched circumstances, meant nothing. The twins were all that mattered and as she stroked her fingertips lightly down Ellie's cheek, causing the moppet to close her eyes and relax, Sheena knew she had to find a way to put aside her past relationship with Will and focus on what needed to be done. Ellie and Sarah were the two people in the world who mattered most to her and she couldn't let them down by becoming a basket case of repressed memories simply because Will was here.

She cleared her throat, still stroking Ellie as her baby fell asleep. 'Have you had much of a chance to look at scans or operation reports? The tissue expanders have worked wonderfully, although the skin took a little longer to stretch than Miles originally thought.'

'Miles has kept me apprised on both of the girls since before they were born.'

'Oh?' She looked at him then, quite surprised. 'I had no idea he'd been in such close contact with you for so long.'

'I was finishing up on another case in Philadelphia. Twin boys who were joined at the spine.'

'Good heavens.' Sheena placed a possessive hand on Ellie's little stomach while the little girl slept alongside her sister. 'Are they all right?'

'Both boys are doing very well. They were almost eight months old when we separated them but now they're fourteen months and both starting to walk around.'

'Wow. That's amazing. Did Miles work with you on that case?'

'Yes. We've worked together many times during the past decade. In fact, it was through working with Miles that I initially entered the field of conjoined twins.' Will paused and frowned for a moment. 'It gave me something new and challenging to focus on.'

Sheena turned away from the crib and took a step towards him. Will immediately drew himself to his full height, his backbone ramrod straight, his defences in place. Although the action may have been involuntary, it told her a lot. This was the man who had been very impor-tant to her all those years ago, the one man in the world who had really understood her, and while they gazed at each other now, she realised that while there still might be an underlying level of attraction simmering beneath the surface, they needed to rise above it, to move past it and to get on with the job at hand.

'Will, I can't thank you enough for coming, for

accepting the job as orthopaedic surgeon to my girls. It means the world to me to know they'll be in such safe hands.'

'They need my expertise. I'm honoured to provide it. It's as cut and dried as that.' His words were clipped and he clenched his jaw. Sheena knew of old that that meant he was either highly uncomfortable, embarrassed or trying to hold on to his temper. In this instance, she wondered whether it wasn't all three.

'I also don't want…' She stopped and laced her fingers together, desperate to keep her composure. 'I mean…I would be horrified to think that you might think that…' She stopped again, biting her lip.

She was nervous and unsure. Will could tell quite clearly from the way she was trying not to wring her hands or bite her lip. It annoyed him that after all this time apart, after everything he'd been through in the past decade, he could still read this woman like a book. It was as though everything about Sheena was burned into his memory and would remain with him for ever.

'We have a past,' he jumped in, saving her the trouble of expressing what he could see clearly written all over her face. His words were spoken in a clipped and firm tone that indicated he'd made a decision and was following through with it. 'We were together—so we know each other well. Things didn't work out. We moved on.' He smoothed a hand down his silk tie before shoving both hands into the pockets of his trousers. 'Now, purely for professional reasons, our paths are once more crossing. We're both very different people now.'

'You're right.' She nodded. 'I mean, you have a life I know nothing about and I have…well, I have the girls to think about.'

'What about your ex-husband? Doesn't he figure in the life of your daughters? Despite what may or may not have happened within your marriage, I had at least expected to see him here, helping you.'

'Er…no.'

Will shook his head as though disagreeing with her. 'The parents' marital problems don't figure at all in the equation of the actual separation of conjoined twins. It's the babies that matter most.'

'I couldn't agree more.'

'So where is he?' He was still frowning, as though not really wanting to talk about this but still wanting to get things completely straight.

'He's gone. Out of my life. Wants nothing to do with the girls.'

Will's expression eased to one of professional concern. 'You're all alone? A single parent?'

'I am.' Her voice wavered as she said the words and there was deep sadness in her eyes. Was it regret for her defunct marriage? All Will knew was that when she stood there, looking up at him, her blue eyes wide and sad with the corner of her lower lip caught between her teeth, he had to remain strong.

Years ago, he'd loved this woman completely. She'd been vitally important to his life but that time was long past. He wasn't responsible for protecting her any more. Neither was he responsible for her happiness. He couldn't allow himself to become ensnared by her again.

Balling his hands into fists in order to stop

himself from going to her, Will breathed deeply before nodding once and turning on his heel. He was only here for the babies, not their mother. Yet, as he walked out of the room, he was positive he could feel her watching his every move.

CHAPTER THREE

THAT evening, after Sheena had fed and changed the girls, tucking them in so they were ready for their evening sleep, she said goodnight to the night sister and made her way from the ward to the hospital's residential wing.

It was close to midnight, the hospital corridors all but deserted, and she looked forward to getting to her small apartment. She knew she could get a good five to six hours' sleep before the girls woke, ready for their breakfast. They were both so lovely, so special and so perfect. Other people might look at the girls and see twins who were joined at the hip but when she looked at them, she saw only Ellie and Sarah, two different little girls, and she loved them completely.

What she longed for most at the moment was to be able to hold them and cuddle them without needing help to get them in and out of the crib.

As it was, with the tissue expanders still in, it only made holding them even more difficult, but there was no way she was giving up her cuddles, even if it probably drove the staff around the twist because she needed help each time. Tomorrow the tissue expanders would come out and then early on Monday morning the surgery to separate them, which Miles estimated would take a good twenty hours—maybe more—would begin.

Her girls. Her babies. They'd lived in the hospital all their lives and so knew nothing different, but she did. She was their mother and she was determined to provide for them both, to give them the best chance at life. Still, Miles had already discussed the pros and cons of the impending surgery with her. They all knew the risks, but to leave the twins as conjoined would cause them not only psychological complications but health complications as well. They all knew that separating the girls was the right course of action to take but still…she was their mother and if anything should happen to either one of them…

Sheena stopped walking, trembling with sudden fear, the burning need to just hold her babies one by one overwhelming her. Tears threatened and she closed them, instantly trying to regain a hold over her emotions, calming her mind down, at least until she managed to get back to the privacy of her room. Leaning a hand against the wall, she swallowed over the lump in her throat.

'Sheena?'

She whirled round at the sound of her name, startled at being discovered and very surprised to find Will standing in the corridor not far from her. Sheena quickly straightened, dropping her hand and sniffing, pulling herself together.

'Will. Is there something I can help you with? You look lost.'

'I am. I was looking for the cafeteria.'

She nodded. 'You've come down one extra floor. The cafeteria is directly above us.' She impatiently blinked the impending tears away, unable to believe that Will, of all people, had caught her at a weak moment. 'There won't be any food on offer, just coffee.'

He nodded but didn't move. He should just turn, walk to the stairwell and leave her alone. He should keep his distance but it was clear she was upset. He'd never been able to resist Sheena when she'd been sad. The need to cheer her up, to support her, was powerful and one he couldn't ignore. Whatever had happened between them in the past could be put aside, at least for a short while.

'Are there any restaurants open outside the hospital? Preferably close? Food would be appreciated. My stomach kept growling all through that last meeting.' He gave her a sheepish smile and Sheena wished he hadn't. He was far too adorable, far too irresistible when he looked at her like that.

'Wow, that meeting ran very late.'

'You're telling me,' he scoffed. 'Restaurants? Any thoughts?'

Glad of the distraction, she mentally went through the restaurants close by. 'Um…there are a few places still open at this time of night. Two Italian restaurants and also a vegetarian café. Ah, but I've just remembered that you're not a big vegetarian fan, so I guess it'll be Italian for you.'

'Well, if you've remembered that I don't like vegetarian food, you'll also remember that I don't like to eat alone. Come on. Let's go.' He started walking towards the door at the end of the corridor, closing the distance between them. 'Are the Italian places within walking distance or do we need to take a taxi?'

Her eyes widened at his words. 'Wait. I can't go with you. I'm going to bed.'

Will stopped beside her and looked down into her upturned face. 'I'm willing to bet you haven't had a proper meal for at least three to four days. Am I right?'

'Yes.'

'It's settled, then.' He smiled and her heart almost skipped a beat. Good heavens, he was even more handsome than he'd been a decade ago. Her heart started pounding a little faster, the earthy, fresh scent she'd always equated with Will teasing her senses once more.

'But, Will...'

He rolled his eyes and shook his head, somewhat bemused. 'It's just dinner, Sheena. Not a lifelong contract, and the longer you argue with me, the later you'll get to sleep, and if I know you, which I do, you'll be back on the ward bright and early to accompany the girls to Theatre.'

Sheena bristled a little at his words, annoyed that he'd made valid points. It *wasn't* a lifelong contract. It *was* just dinner and she *was* hungry. 'Of course I'll be on the ward. They *are* my girls. It's my responsibility to care for them.'

'And it's my present responsibility to eat. Let's go, Woodcombe.' He placed his hand beneath her elbow and urged her towards the door.

Sheena pulled her arm free of his grasp, heat burning through her at where he'd touched her. 'I'm coming. No need to manhandle me, Beckman.'

'I'm hungry. Let's hustle.'

'You always were bad-tempered when you needed food.' They walked outside into the cool October air and Sheena now wished she'd brought her cardigan instead of leaving it in the girls' room. Then again, she hadn't expected to be leaving the hospital to have dinner with Will Beckman.

They walked through the hospital grounds, the silence around them starting to grow tense and a little uncomfortable. In order to help her flustered nerves, which he'd had the audacity to ruffle, Sheena found herself pointing out different buildings as they walked along. It was strange to be making small talk with Will but, then, in many respects, he *was* a stranger.

'That's the pathology building and down that way is the medical school. That large building is the administration building and this,' she said as they walked past a small brick chapel, 'is where I like to come and just think, to just ponder, to just stop.'

Will looked at the little chapel with its white-painted door, brown bricks and the little steeple on top. 'A place of solitude.'

Sheena shrugged. 'We all need one.'

As soon as they reached the roadside, where the taxi rank was situated, Will walked to the first taxi and held the door open for Sheena.

'Where ya headed?' the driver asked them as

Sheena sat in the back, trying to keep her distance from Will.

'Giuseppe's, please,' she told him, and a moment later they were driving through the streets of Adelaide at midnight.

'Wow. Everything looks just as I remembered. The country town trying to be a big city.' He smiled as he said the words.

Sheena frowned. 'Don't some of your family live here? I can't remember.'

'My parents and one sister. She's married with children and lives just around the corner from my parents.'

'I'll bet your parents are glad to have you home for a while.'

He nodded. 'They are.'

Sheena sighed, her tone wistful. 'I always envied your family. Whenever you spoke about them, it always sounded so…wonderful. Lots of siblings, lots of mischief.' She nodded to herself. 'That's what I want for my girls…well, the mischief part at any rate.'

She looked down at her hands, surprised to find they were shaking. 'Right now, though, I just want them to be healthy.' She swallowed over the lump in her throat.

'The projected outcomes for the surgery are good, Sheena.' Will placed a hand over hers, needing to offer her hope.

'I know.' She forced a smile. 'It's never easy for a mother when her child is sick or needs surgery. Over the years, I've watched the parents of my little patients as their child was wheeled away to surgery and the devastation and fear and pain and anguish reflected in their eyes is now permanently lodged in my throat.'

'We have a great team together and Miles knows what he's doing.'

Sheena quickly shook her head. 'I'm not concerned about the team. I know everyone will do everything they can for my girls. I'm confident with that. What I'm not confident about are these maternal emotions. I never thought I'd have them and now that I do, they're…intense.'

'In a way, I envy you.' Will's words were soft and he dropped his hand from her shoulder. 'You're a parent. You have children. That's special.'

Sheena looked at him. 'It is special.' Her words were a whisper then she cleared her throat, asking the question that had been burning through her since the wedding. 'You've never met...anyone else? I'm not trying to pry, Will,' she rushed on hurriedly.

'Sure you are,' he countered, thoughts of Beatrice coming to his mind. He and Beatrice were well and truly over, had been for the past two years, but he had to admit he would feel strange telling Sheena about his aborted engagement. 'But why shouldn't you? Why shouldn't I? I've already told you I'm curious about you and I'm determined to get answers.'

'You deserve them.' She nodded. 'We can clear the air tonight. Start afresh tomorrow.'

'Just like that?' He was a little surprised at her words. 'One hundred per cent honesty?'

'Yes.'

The taxi slowed before he could say anything more and soon they were climbing out and paying the driver. Neither of them spoke as they were welcomed by one of the waiters and led to a table. Sheena waved to the few other patrons in the restaurant, all of whom worked at Adelaide Mercy.

'How are the girls tonight?' one woman asked. Sheena recognised her as one of the dieticians and smiled politely.

'Growing more and more every day.'

'Good to hear.'

'You're well known,' Will said, after she'd been asked a few more questions. He held out her chair for her and waited until she was seated before sitting down opposite her.

'I'm the mother of Adelaide's conjoined twins, a minor celebrity.' She spoke with forced joviality, then sighed and shrugged. 'I've become used to it, especially at work.'

'The press don't bother you?'

'Charisma, Adelaide Mercy's CEO, and the rest of the PR department take care of those things. Apart from when the girls were born, I haven't really been hounded. The PR department discuss the information with me and give their recommendations, such as which journalists to speak to and who to stay clear of, but other than that things haven't been too bad. My main focus is to look after the girls.'

'That's good to hear. Many parents of conjoined children are often hounded by the media for photographs and update reports. You do know that things will heat up again with the impending separation surgery?'

Sheena nodded and sipped at the glass of water the waiter had just poured for her, declining the offer of wine as she was still expressing milk for the twins. 'Miles took me through the drill.'

'Good.' Will opened the menu and after a moment of perusing it gave his order to the waiter, as did Sheena, and once he'd left them alone, Sheena put both hands on the table and leaned forward a little, not wanting her voice to travel to the other patrons.

'Shall we begin?' It all seemed so strange, so civilised but Sheena rationalised this was probably better than ranting and raving and getting way too emotional. Calm and controlled. Open and honest. It seemed the best way to proceed.

'Now?'

'Why not? You go first. Ask away.'

Will nodded then jumped right in. 'When you rejected my proposal, were you telling the truth about not being able to have children?'

Sheena tried not to wince at his accusatory tone and tried not to take it to heart. Will had obviously thought about this as his question had rolled immediately off his tongue with no hesitation whatsoever. She'd agreed to provide him with answers and she was going to follow through. If there was any hope that she and Will could find some common ground, that they could put the past behind them and hopefully become friends, it would be good not only for them but for the girls as well. She would do *anything* for her girls and if it meant being uncomfortable whilst sorting things out, then it would all be worth it.

She swallowed and nodded. 'Yes. I had bad endometriosis. The chances of me conceiving were, I was told, impossible.'

'And yet you have twins.'

'And yet I have twins,' she agreed, that same secret smile touching her lips. 'Miracle twins.' She breathed the two words as though they were her heart and soul. Will found that puzzling yet interesting.

'So if you knew you couldn't have children, why did you marry?'

Her expression changed, a small frown furrowing her brow. 'Jonas didn't want children. He was a plastic surgeon I met at a paediatric conference on facial reconstruction. We hit it off, started dating and I was determined not to make the same mistakes I'd made with you. So I told him upfront that I was unable to have children and he was happy about it. He'd said he was focused on his career, that he had expensive tastes and that children didn't fit into his life at all. We were…compatible, and so when he proposed I accepted.' She looked down at her hands, clasped together in front of her, trying not to feel highly self-conscious at discussing her marriage with Will.

'When my gynaecological surgeon contacted me about a new surgical technique of removing the endometrial cysts from my ovaries, I was interested. He said it would alleviate a lot of my pain.'

Will was surprised to hear her speak of pain. 'Were you always in pain? I don't remember you ever complaining of abdominal pain.'

Sheena laughed without humour. 'When you've had the pain for most of your life, you learn to deal with it. Anyway, the surgery worked. The pain was dramatically reduced and then two months after the surgery, when I returned for an ultrasound, it was discovered I was pregnant. Naturally I was over the moon and I thought Jonas would be, too.'

'He really didn't want the children?'

She shook her head. 'He really didn't. He said I'd lied to him, telling him I could never have children and then conceiving only twelve months after we were married. He said I'd violated our prenuptial agreement and that it was grounds for divorce. Within the week he'd contacted his solicitor, packed up my belongings and made me leave the house.'

'He kicked you out!' Will couldn't help but see red at some other man treating any woman in such a fashion, let alone Sheena. 'That's disgusting.'

Sheena shrugged and sighed. 'He was well within his legal rights. Besides, at least he was honest. At least he didn't pretend he was happy when he wasn't, unlike my parents.'

'*Your* parents?'

'My parents are very wealthy, very prominent solicitors in Sydney.'

'They're alive? I'd always thought they'd passed away as you never spoke of them.' He shook his head. Why didn't he know all of this? The two of them had been so close, or so he'd thought.

'We don't talk. We haven't spoken in…' She paused for a moment as she tried to calculate. 'Well over two decades—ever since my fourteenth birthday. I was at boarding school and had been told by my teacher that my parents were supposed to pick me up and take me out for the day. They never showed. I called the house, worried that they might have had an accident, that something bad might have happened, but I was told by Harrington, our butler, that my parents had flown overseas that morning on urgent business and wouldn't be back for six months.'

She looked down at her hands and gave a small shrug. 'They'd forgotten me—again. I didn't hear from them during the rest of my time at boarding school. Then, as soon as I turned eighteen, their contract—as they called it—with me expired and I was told by one of their solicitor colleagues hired to handle my "case" that I was on my own.'

'Oh, Sheena.' Will felt her pain and wanted to be there for her, to touch her, to let her know how disturbed he was to learn of her past. He wasn't entirely sure what sort of reaction from him was appropriate when rehashing the past with an old girlfriend…so he sat and waited for her to continue.

'Apparently, when my mother discovered she was pregnant with me, she said she felt as though her world had come to an end. My father wasn't interested in her any more because she was large and fat—her words, not mine.'

Sheena shook her head, trying not to feel hurt and betrayed, but she couldn't help it. After all these years, the cold, impersonal way in which she'd been raised still had the ability to hurt her.

It also made her determined *never* to do that to *her* girls. 'She even once told me that if the doctor who had first confirmed her pregnancy hadn't been part of their social set, she would have had an abortion. However, she couldn't deal with the possibility of being ostracised by her friends, most of whom had the odd child or two, so she decided to continue with the pregnancy.'

'What? How old were you when she told you that?'

'Seven. I remember asking her why she never came to see me at boarding school, why she never attended the school concerts I took part in, why I was driven to and from school by a chauffeur rather than my father. Of course, I had no idea what the word *abortion* meant so I asked my teachers.'

'I had no idea.' He shook his head. 'Why didn't you tell me any of this before? How come I don't know this about you?' It also made him wonder whether he'd been so wrapped up in creating his own perfect family picture that he hadn't bothered to dig a little deeper where Sheena was concerned.

She shrugged. 'I didn't talk about it at all. Period. My parents didn't share a caring bone in their bodies—except perhaps for each other, and even then I'm not so sure. My mother demanded a C-section delivery, simply because she refused to give birth naturally, and then when she'd regained her pre-pregnancy figure my father started paying her attention again. I was only endured because to do otherwise would have brought ridicule from their elitist friends. To them, having "offspring" was considered acceptable, even though they didn't raise me.'

Will thought for a moment, recalling some of the conversations they'd had or, more correctly, the times he'd talked about his family, not realising that Sheena had *never* talked of hers. 'And then there was me. Always going on about my parents and my siblings and my nieces and nephews.'

'You didn't go on.' She smiled. 'I loved hearing your stories. I loved them so much and I could tell that family was so very important to you. You *needed* children, Will, so you *needed* a wife who could give you that.' She shook her head sadly. 'That wasn't me.'

'So you turned me down. Instead of talking to me, instead of sharing with me, instead of trusting me, you simply decided to run away?'

'Hey, I didn't run away. It was extremely difficult for me to do what needed to be done. I was raised in a non-communicative household and then a boarding school so I've never been any good at talking about my feelings, but I didn't run away from you.' She tried not to raise her voice, to keep her tone on that calm, even footing she wanted, but it was difficult when he was accusing her.

Will shook his head. 'No. Not buying it. Those may have been the reasons you *told* yourself you couldn't accept me but deep down inside you were scared. I can see that now. You were scared of opening up, of getting close to someone. You probably thought that one day I would slap you down the way everyone else around you had done, and so you rejected me before I could reject you. A pre-emptive strike.'

Sheena knew his words were close to the truth.

She *had* been scared, scared that he would one day come to really hate her…and she hadn't been able to live with even the thought of that. 'Or that if I'd said yes, if I'd accepted your proposal and we'd got married, you would have eventually come to hate me for not being able to give you the one thing you've always wanted—a great big happy family.

'And if you *had* married me, those gorgeous girls wouldn't just be yours, they'd be ours. *Our* miracle. Instead, they belong to another man… another man who doesn't even want them.' The last words were said with utter disgust.

'Which is why I intend to give them all the love I have and more. Those girls are my life and I will do anything and everything to ensure their health and happiness. Even when I had a lot of bleeding early on in the pregnancy and even when I had to stay bedridden, feeling as though I had no other purpose in life than to be a human incubator, nothing else mattered other than giving my babies everything I had to give. From the instant I was told about them, I've loved them with every fibre of my being. And

I shall continue to be there for them, to provide them with a happy home for the rest of my life.' Vehemence laced her tone, pride stiffened her backbone and determination was written all over her face.

When the waiter arrived with their food, his presence almost startled her and she realised she'd become too intensely focused on herself and Will. The rest of the restaurant came back into focus—the sights, the smells, the surroundings. The waiter smiled politely, wished them a brief *'Buon appetito'* then left them alone once more.

Will quietly picked up his fork and twirled it into his pasta before lifting it to his lips. 'Mmm,' he said a moment later. 'Delicious. Good choice of restaurant, Sheena.'

That was it? Wasn't he going to ask any more questions or had he discovered all the answers he needed? Confusion swam through her and as she started to calm down, she realised the waiter had unfurled her napkin and placed it in her lap. An uncomfortable silence started to settle over them and Sheena wasn't sure what to say to alleviate it.

'Why don't the girls have your husband's surname?' Will asked after a few minutes, his words so abrupt that Sheena almost dropped her fork to her plate. 'I've noticed on their charts that they're both listed as Woodcombe.'

Sheena shrugged. 'As Jonas wasn't interested in the girls and as I hadn't changed my name when we married, it seemed ridiculous for us to have different surnames.'

'You didn't change your name.' He pondered the words, intrigued that she'd chosen to remain a Woodcombe given that she had no ties to her family heritage. Had that been because the process was too time consuming, or because deep down inside she'd known her marriage to Jonas would never last?

'My medical degree is in the name of Sheena Woodcombe. Whether or not I'd changed it, I'd still have to practice as Dr Woodcombe. It just seemed simpler to leave things as they were.'

'It didn't bother your ex-husband?'

'No. Why? Would it bother you?'

Will pondered her words for a moment then leaned forward a little. 'Not that it has anything to do with our present situation, but if we'd been married, would you have changed your name?'

Sheena nodded, her decision almost instant, as though at some point she'd given it some thought. 'More than likely. Besides, when we were together I was still a registrar and didn't have my paediatric consultant qualifications.'

'So it's all logistics to you?'

'I've had to be logical. It was the only defence I had against the way I was raised. Closing myself off, being logical about all things was the only way I could cope. Janessa was the first person ever to break through my barriers…and…' She took a calming breath, reminding herself that she was being completely honest with him to-night. 'And you were second.'

'And what about Jonas? Was he the third?'

'No. Jonas never broke through my barriers. I loved him but it was more companionship. A marriage I could be in so that I had someone to share things with, to discuss my day with. Mar-riage is all about someone else being a witness to your life and at that time I was very lonely. I had Janessa and I had my work and that was it.' She shook her head. 'I don't expect you to understand as you have a plethora of siblings and loving, caring parents who are actually interested in your life, who *want* to talk to you, who *want* to spend time with you.'

'I do understand, Sheena.' He nodded slowly. 'I've been living overseas for well over a decade now and although I am in contact with my parents, they don't know much about my life. About the way I'm always working to stave off loneliness.'

'You've been lonely?' Sheena's heart started to ache for him, to ache for this man who had meant so much to her.

'Don't sound so surprised, Sheena. Loneliness can happen to people even if they have a big family around them. Being an only child to indifferent parents doesn't give you a monopoly on the emotion.'

'Uh…' She shook her head. 'No. I never meant to imply that it did.' She bit her lip and asked again the question she'd asked during the taxi ride to the restaurant. 'Didn't you…? I mean…I thought you would have met someone else. I thought by now that you would be married with that large family you always wanted.'

Will looked down at his food and placed his fork on the side of his plate, lifting his gaze to give Sheena his full attention. He'd asked about her and she'd replied. It was only fair that he do the same.

'I did meet someone else. Beatrice. We met through work. She was a lawyer advising on a medico-legal case I was involved with. We dated, became engaged and then…' He stopped and shook his head. 'I broke it off. We were heading off to the printer to do a final check on the invitations as they were due to be sent out the following day and I…' He stopped again and ran a hand over his face as though he couldn't believe what had transpired.

'It *felt* wrong. I can't explain it any other way. Everything about the wedding, about spending the rest of my life with Beatrice, just felt… wrong.' He could still hear Beatrice telling him that he spent more time at work than with her.

That work was his first priority whereas *she* should have been. He had known that that would never change.

He was dedicated to his job and, as he'd told Sheena at the wedding, it made him happy. He'd buried himself in work when Sheena had left and it had taken quite a few years for him to start dating again. Finally, though, he'd been able to move on and when he'd met Beatrice, he'd thought he'd once more found happiness.

He'd been wrong…again.

Will cleared his throat. 'I knew I couldn't enter into a marriage with doubts and I realised that Beatrice deserved better than me. She deserved someone who would worship the ground she walked on, who would be there for her at the end of a hard day's work, someone who could spend their weekends with her.'

He picked up his wineglass and twirled the liquid, looking into it but not seeing it at all. Sheena watched him closely. He was miles away. She could see the pain in his eyes and in his furrowed brow as he recalled his past.

'I was always being called away to an emergency or would be stuck late in Theatre or would be in meetings or on call over the weekend. I was often either interstate or overseas consulting on different cases, especially with conjoined twins. It completely frustrated her. I guess in the end it all took its toll because I could see Beatrice was coming to resent my job, even though she admired my dedication.' He put the glass down without taking a sip. 'That was when I came to the conclusion that she deserved better.'

'It's difficult doing the right thing—especially when it tears you up inside.' Sheena spoke softly, remembering the way she'd felt when she'd turned down Will's proposal, knowing that he deserved better. Even now, sitting across the table from him all these years later, she still felt the pain of that day. 'I'm sorry it didn't work out for you, Will. Truly I am.' There was deep sincerity in her tone.

Before he could reply, a man approached their table.

'I heard you were in my restaurant and I had to come and say hello to the beautiful mother. It is good to see you in here and not be sending you takeaway.' The elderly Italian, suave and debonair, pulled Sheena to her feet and kissed both of her cheeks soundly.

'It's good to be here, Giuseppe.' Sheena smiled at the man, genuinely pleased to see him.

'And the babies? They are fine? Growing big? I am sorry that I have not been in to see them more. Business has been busy.'

'Don't you worry about it. The girls are both growing big but visitors will be restricted for the next month or so.' She glanced at Will, then back to the proprietor. 'Their surgery will start soon.' There was a hint of anxiety in her tone. Will was sure Giuseppe hadn't picked up on it, but he could tell. It appeared that talking about the major surgical operation caused Sheena quite a bit of distress—and rightly so. The lives of her baby girls would be in jeopardy. While the assembled teams responsible for the surgery were all experts and were all doing every test possible to avoid complications, sometimes unforeseen problems arose.

'In fact,' she continued, 'please allow me to introduce you to the leading orthopaedic surgeon on the case, Will Beckman.'

Will stood and held out his hand to the restaurateur.

'Ah. Dr Will. I have heard Miles talk of you.' Giuseppe disregarded Will's proffered hand and instead grabbed him by the shoulders, leaning up to kiss him on both cheeks. 'You are most welcome to my humble restaurant and, please, you must accept that you are my guests this late evening.'

When both of them started to protest, he held up his hands. 'I insist. I will leave you now. You no doubt have much to discuss, but remember— when you are at that hospital and you are hungry, you call Giuseppe and I will prepare you fresh food and send it straight away.'

'Thank you.' Sheena leaned over and kissed his cheek. 'You're a good man.'

'And we will have Ellie's and Sarah's first birthday party here,' he declared. 'It will be bigger and better than Miles's and Janessa's wedding reception.' He placed a hand to the side of his mouth and said in a stage whisper, 'But we won't tell Miles and Janessa that.' Letting out a large belly laugh, Giuseppe headed back towards the kitchen.

'He's jovial, isn't he?' Will stated rhetorically as they sat back down.

'He is.'

'So this is where Miles and Janessa had their reception. I was sorry I had to leave early.'

'Everyone understood, Will. You had a sick patient to care for. Miles was thrilled you'd made it to the ceremony, so was Janessa, but this place looked like something out of a romantic fairy-tale. Giuseppe and his staff had hung twinkle lights around the room with big bouquets of flowers on each table. Crisp white tablecloths, white covers with big red bows on the chairs...' She trailed off and slowly shook her head. 'He really outdid himself.' Sheena sighed, wistful and relaxed, even if it was for just a moment.

Will couldn't help but watch her. Outwardly she'd changed but only slightly. Her hair was much shorter now than when they'd been to-gether and where he'd loved her long hair, he couldn't get over how perfect the short cut, as her hair bounced and curled slightly around her face, suited her. Dark hair, pale skin, blue eyes, pink lips. That was Sheena.

'Giuseppe's a good man,' she continued as she took a sip of her water. 'Genuine, too.'

'That's an odd comment to make.'

'Not really. The hospital has been contacted by so many different firms. People who sell baby clothes, baby furniture, baby toys, all wanting me to use their products with the twins so they can give a "used by Adelaide's own conjoined twins Ellie and Sarah Woodcombe" endorsement. It's quite ridiculous.'

'But I'll bet you've stood your ground and didn't endorse a single product, right?'

'Right.'

'And yet you're more than happy for Giuseppe to organise, six months in advance, the girls' first birthday party?'

'If he wants to. As I've said, he's genuine. He cares about what happens to my girls, and to me. It's nice. He's not in it for the publicity.'

Will finished his last mouthful and dabbed at his mouth with a napkin. 'Are you sure?'

'Definitely. I have to believe I'm still a good judge of character.'

Was she talking about him? Did she not trust her judgement where he was concerned? 'You've had reason to question it?'

Sheena shrugged carelessly and pushed her plate away, her food only half-eaten. 'My divorce was finalised three months ago, Will, so, yes, you could say that I've had reason to question it.'

'Fair enough.' The wistfulness had disappeared from her eyes and he could tell she was getting more and more tired with each passing moment. He wanted to see happiness light her features again, to listen to her talk with optimism and spirit. He offered her dessert or a coffee but she turned both down and suggested they call it a night.

They said goodbye to Giuseppe and thanked him for their meals, taking another ten minutes just to get out of the restaurant, but when they were in the taxi, heading back to the hospital, Sheena leaned her head back against the seat, her eyes closed.

'Tell me more about Miles's and Janessa's reception,' Will said softly.

'Why?'

He shrugged. 'I wasn't there. You were.'

'They have the whole thing on DVD.'

Will exhaled with resignation. 'You know I hate sitting down and watching those things.'

She opened her eyes, giving him a small smile. 'I remember.'

'I'd much rather hear about it from you.'

'OK, but you still might not be able to get out of sitting down and watching the whole two-hour DVD—with running commentary from both Miles and Janessa.' She chuckled and when they arrived back at the hospital allowed him to hold the door for her. She was tired, and as they walked along she tripped, her feet tired and clumsy, but Will was there to steady her, leaving one arm about her waist afterwards.

She talked softly, telling him about the reception and how Miles hadn't been able to keep his eyes or his hands off his bride. 'I've never seen Janessa or Miles so happy, and even now, three months on, they're both still ecstatic.'

'Yes. It is nice.'

The entire time she talked and the entire time he listened, she was acutely aware of the way his arm hovered lightly at her waist, supporting her in her exhausted state in case she stumbled again. When she shivered due to the very early morning breeze, he quickly slipped off his suit jacket and placed it around her shoulders. She wished he hadn't because then his scent only encompassed her even more.

She wasn't even quite sure what she was saying any more, her mind sluggishly trying to recall events that had happened at her best friend's wedding. All she was aware of was his nearness, his arm at her waist, his jacket around her shoulders. His scent, his touch, his heat. It flowed through her, bringing dormant parts of her that she'd buried way down deep pulsating back to life.

As they entered the residential wing, Sheena stopped walking and Will dropped his arm as she turned to face him. 'Anyway, this is where I'm staying. It's lodgers only past this point, I'm afraid. If you came in, you'd need to sign the register and give proof of identification, and it's all too much rigmarole for this time of night.'

'Early morning,' he corrected, as she slid his suit jacket from her shoulders and handed it back with thanks.

She shrugged and crossed her arms over her chest, both as a means of guarding herself from him but also to help her keep warm after the loss of his jacket. 'I guess I'll see you in the morning.'

'I guess you will.'

She paused. 'Thanks again for dinner…and the chat. I hope I've been able to put your mind at rest, to give you the answers you were looking for.'

'In a way, yes. I think I've realised tonight that ten years ago I didn't know you as well as I thought I did. Perhaps, when you turned me down, you did do the right thing after all.'

'Oh.' Why was it that his words pierced her heart and made her feel bereft? Standing here, looking at him, and now being the mother of two gorgeous girls, she wished on all the wishes in the world that she could go back in time and *accept* his proposal. They would have been married, she would have had the surgery and she would have conceived *his* children, and they all would have lived happily ever after.

But that wasn't the way things had turned out. To all intents and purposes they were strangers…strangers who shared a past.

CHAPTER FOUR

ON FRIDAY, the tissue expanders were removed, Miles and Janessa more than happy with the way the girls were handling the preparation for their up-and-coming long surgical procedure. Today was Sunday and the girls had just returned from the radiology department, where they'd undergone yet another scan. Their surgery was scheduled for the following morning and tensions were high.

Sheena knew it was all necessary and that the more information the surgeons had before the big day the better, but each time the girls needed scans they had to be anaesthetised and Sarah always woke up grouchy.

Sarah shifted in the crib, accidentally kicking Ellie, and by the time the porters had wheeled the crib back onto the paediatric ward, both girls were crying.

'Oh, I know. I know,' she crooned to both of them, quickly settling the crib and touching both of their cheeks. She pressed kisses to Ellie's forehead and then to Sarah's, but both girls cried on, part sleepy, part annoyed and part hungry.

'It's all right. Mummy's here. I'll get your bottles.' She pressed the buzzer on the wall, indicating she needed some help from one of the staff. The girls couldn't be left alone while she went off to get bottles of her expressed milk, which were stored in a fridge in the staffroom, especially as they were still coming around from an anaesthetic.

Raquel-Maria stuck her head around the door. 'Bottles?'

'Yes, please.' When she'd left, Sheena pressed a hand to her breasts, feeling the let-down pain of milk release, which often happened around the girls' feed time. It would mean that she would soon need to express some more milk, and while she knew it was the best thing for her babies, to be drinking her milk complete with antibodies, she had to admit she often felt like a cow at milking time.

'But you're worth it,' she crooned to the two of them, still kissing them and whispering to them in a quiet and controlled voice.

'I hear it's feeding time,' a deep voice said from the doorway, and when Sheena looked up, she saw Will standing there, holding two ready-to-drink bottles of expressed milk.

'Yes. What are you doing here?'

'Checking on my patients. Raquel-Maria told me to bring these to you so I guess I'm also helping with the feeding.'

Sarah started to cry even harder and it didn't matter whether Sheena liked having Will in the room to help out or not, the girls needed feeding.

'Help me raise the crib so it's at an angle—they feed better that way.'

Will nodded, put both bottles down on the table and helped Sheena to turn the handles located on either side of the crib, which then angled the entire mattress, making it easier to feed the girls.

Sheena had only seen him sporadically since their impromptu dinner the other night. She knew the theatre team, which included Will, had been meeting for hours on end to go over every aspect of the surgery. He'd been around several times to assess the girls but at no point had he referred to their conversation at dinner. She hoped that meant he'd received the answers he'd been looking for and that they could keep their relationship professional and focused on the girls. Sheena needed all her mental strength to cope with what was happening tomorrow.

'You take Ellie. I'll do Sarah. She's already starting to work herself up and if she doesn't feed properly, she'll be sick.'

Will agreed and quickly tested both bottles by shaking a few drops from each onto his wrist, ensuring the milk was the correct temperature before handing one bottle to Sheena. She went round to the right side of the crib, bending over Sarah a bit more. 'Shh, darling. Mummy's here. Mummy's here. It's OK. Everything's OK,' she crooned softly, and ever so slightly Sarah's cries started to subside.

Sheena bent her finger and put her knuckle near Sarah's mouth to initiate the sucking reflex and the baby quietened a bit more. With a lightning-quick move, she swapped her knuckle for the teat of the bottle before Sarah could pro-test and, with Ellie already drinking the bottle Will was holding, the room was soon plunged into a welcome silence.

'That's better,' she said with a sigh, trying her best to stop Sarah from guzzling the milk.

'She certainly has a good set of lungs on her,' Will murmured, a half-smile on his lips.

'That's for certain.' They both fell silent, lis-tening to the girls drinking from their bottles with little murmuring noises of satisfaction.

'Are you looking forward to them starting solids?'

'Most definitely, they're growing so rapidly. While they were quite small when they were born, they weren't as small as Janessa first feared, and both of them have fantastic appetites. A nice five and a half pounds for Sarah and five pounds for Ellie.'

'That *is* quite good for twins. You said you were bedridden for the last few months of your pregnancy.'

'It was safer for the girls. There was no way I was going to miscarry, and with being in hospital…well, I didn't have anywhere to live anyway so it was best for all.'

'Do you have somewhere to live now?'

'Not anywhere outside the hospital. It seemed pointless to be paying rent or a mortgage when I'm spending all my time here. There are nights when I sleep in this room and other nights when I sleep in the residential wing. I've recently gone back to consulting a few half-days per week in the clinic and, quite frankly, finding somewhere to live isn't a high priority at the moment.' She stroked Sarah's cheek, maternal love in her voice as she spoke. 'The girls need me here.'

Will agreed with her sentiments but it seemed odd to him that she had no place she could call home. She was a strong woman. He'd always known that about her, but to see her like this, alone in the world, a single mother without the support of her parents, about to face an emotionally taxing forty-eight hours with her daughters' impending surgery, only highlighted just how strong she was.

'Everyone needs roots, Sheena.'

'And that's what I'm doing for my girls.

They're going to be in hospital for at least the next three months and then I'll buy a house, put down roots and start my own happy home. I want to have that perfect, fairy-tale family life you often talked about. I want the laughter and silly little squabbles and the making up and the sorting out. I want Sarah and Ellie to have the type of home life I always dreamed of but never had.'

Will pondered her words for a moment, reflecting on the squabbles he'd had with his brothers and sisters—the loud family dinners, the strict rules and regulations his parents had enforced, all designed to love and protect their brood. It was what he'd wanted, that idyllic picture of family, and Sheena intended to paint her own version…without a father for her girls.

He knew she could do it. He knew she would struggle and be severely challenged along the way and the briefest part of him wanted to be around to help and to advise and be challenged alongside her…but he knew that was impossible.

While Ellie and Sarah were indeed gorgeous girls, they weren't his. He hadn't come to

Australia to play father figure to another man's children. He'd come as a surgeon, one responsible for leading the team of highly skilled orthopods in the separation procedure of the twins. He looked down at Ellie, who had almost finished her bottle, her face relaxed in contented pleasure, her stomach full, completely unaware of what awaited her.

The next day might well be the biggest day of her young life but she didn't know it. She was small and helpless and trusting. What if, when she grew up, she trusted the wrong person? What if someone teased her or bullied her at school? What if she fell in love with a boy who didn't love her back?

Will swallowed over the instant need to protect her—not only Ellie but Sarah as well. These girls had no father figure in their life, not even a grandfather who could step in and provide guidance.

But these weren't his children. He had to keep reminding himself of that.

Will removed the bottle when Ellie finished feeding, looking over at Sarah who had also finished. She lay there, wriggling her feet and hands a little, her big blue eyes wide open, eyes that were exactly the same shade as her mother's. He couldn't believe how much the girls looked like Sheena. Even though they were only six months old, they were both incredibly beautiful—as was their mother.

Sheena looked at him and held his gaze, neither of them speaking but both saying a lot with their eyes. Will could see a mixture of confusion and despair behind her brave front. When she bit her lip, he knew she was nervous and worried about something. Well, of course she would be. The next forty-eight hours were going to be some of the most intensely emotional hours she had faced. He wanted to go to her, to hold her, to reassure her, to tell her that everything would be all right, that he and the team of doctors had successfully separated other sets of conjoined twins who had been even more intricately connected than Ellie and Sarah, but he didn't.

Sheena looked away, moving to stand in front of the girls, rubbing and gently patting their chests. Ellie stayed asleep and Sarah started to relax even more, her eyelids starting to flutter closed, getting heavier by the moment.

Sheena started to hum a soft lullaby, the sweet melody filling the small private room. Sarah instantly responded to the sound and soon the twins had successfully slipped back into slumber.

Will allowed her song to wind its way around him. She had such a beautiful voice and the words of love contained in the lyrics were sung with such heartfelt intensity. He could recall his own mother singing to him as a child, the sounds strong and reassuring, and he'd been able to close his eyes and fall asleep secure in the knowledge that with his family around him he would always be safe.

Her voice broke as she finished the song, emotion rising to the fore. The room was plunged into silence as she pulled a blanket over the girls and tucked them in. Then she stepped back, shoved her hands into the pockets of her denim skirt and looked at Will.

'Thanks for your help.' Her tone was thick,

and Will could see her anxiety and concern for her girls was increasing.

'You're welcome.' He shoved his hands deep into his pockets, too. They both stood there, looking at each other, remembering what had attracted them to each other in the first place all those years ago as well as fighting the present attraction, which seemed to weigh heavily about them. 'I'd forgotten just how lovely your voice was.'

Sheena smiled but it didn't reach her eyes. Her lower lip began to wobble. 'It's nice of you to say so.' She clenched her jaw and blinked a few times, trying to hold on to her emotions. Why wasn't he leaving? Why was he just standing there? She was almost at breaking point and a few of the looks he'd given her already had let her know that he had no intention of picking up where they'd left off.

Her breathing rate started to increase and the tears came into her eyes, refusing to be blinked away. 'I don't want to hold you up. You probably have a lot of things to do and organise.' She wiped a hand impatiently across her eyes, sniffing and swallowing over the large lump in her throat. Her chin wobbled again.

'Sheena—' he began, clearly seeing her distress.

'Just…go. Please?'

'You're worried about the girls. That much is evident.' He felt so helpless, standing there with his hands in his pockets. What he wanted desperately was to go to her, to put his arms around her, to comfort her, to help her, as he had so often in the past.

'Of course I'm worried about them. I know you say that everything is going to be all right but—' She broke off, the tears and emotions overcoming her. 'They're my babies. *Mine.*' She looked at him then, tears streaming down her cheeks, lips pursed together between the gasps of air she was dragging into her lungs. 'I never thought I'd ever have children and now that I do, I want to protect them and keep them safe and do everything I can for them and give them the chance of a normal life and…' She let the sentence drift off, hiccuping a little. 'I love them so much, Will,' she said through her tears, 'and if they…if something goes—' She broke off, shaking her head, then whispered between her sobs, 'I'm terrified.'

'Oh, Sheenie,' he ground out, and within the next instant he'd covered the distance that separated them and hauled her into his protective arms.

How on earth was he supposed to resist this woman when she needed him most? He stood firm and held her in his arms, bringing her as close to his body as he dared. Memories flooded through his mind as he breathed in her scents, allowing the essence of Sheena to wash over him. Will closed his eyes, resting his chin lightly on her head as she buried her face into his shirt and continued to cry.

It would be far too easy to slip back into old habits, of thinking about her in a romantic light. That wasn't why he was here and he had to find the strength to at least keep himself one step removed from her…but it was extremely difficult when she was this upset. He tightened his hold on her.

As her sobs began to subside, her breathing became deeper and she settled against his chest, her hands tucked beneath her chin. She wasn't exactly sure how long they stood there but even as the hiccuping became less, Will made no move to pull away. Sheena kept her eyes closed, breathing in the fresh earthy scent that always drove her to distraction.

Feeling his arms about her, being so close to his firm, muscled body, listening to his heart beat beneath his chest…these were the little things in life she'd thought she'd never get the chance to experience again. When she'd rejected his proposal, it had broken her heart. The look of surprise, of disbelief, of complete anguish that had been present in his features, his blue eyes changing from sincere to stormy, had been a sight burned into her memory.

Never again had she thought she'd be enfolded in his arms, drawing comfort from him, but here she was, feeling safe and secure and protected. Her breathing was almost back to normal now and still he made no move to pull away.

Was it the past that was making him stay where he was? Or was it possible that Will had really forgiven her for refusing his proposal and was ready to move on with their friendship? The fact that the underlying attraction between them had never died was clearly evident but she had no idea what it might mean.

She could feel a sneeze starting to build and sniffed, trying to make it go away, twitching her nose to try and get rid of it. She wanted to stay here in Will's arms and not worry about anything else. She pursed her lips, trying to hold back the building sneeze, but knew it wasn't doing any good. A shudder began to ripple through her body and if she didn't pull away from him now and quickly get a tissue…well, it wasn't going to be pretty.

Jerking back, forcing his arms to suddenly let her go, Sheena spun around and all but lunged for the tissue box. She wrenched out a tissue just in time, sneezed and then blew her nose. She tried to blow quietly so as not to wake the girls, and when she was finished she picked up the tissues and turned to put them in the bin—only to find the room empty.

Will had gone…again.

* * *

Will continued to scrub his hands, his mind focused on what lay ahead. Doing his best for his patients was what he'd always done, but this time it was different. This time it was personal and he knew he wasn't the only one in the operating suite who felt the same way. Both Miles and Janessa were here, along with a lot of the other Adelaide Mercy theatre staff.

Of course, there were also staff who had only arrived the day before, such as Marta von Hugen, a colleague from Philadelphia, with whom both he and Miles had worked with on several occasions. Marta would be in charge of the second team of specialists as surgery of this magnitude meant that staff worked on a rotating basis. Ensuring the health and alertness of all involved with such extensive surgery was of paramount importance.

Will looked at the scans that were up on the viewing box in the theatre room. He'd studied them so completely that he felt he knew every inch of them. As far as the operation went, he'd been faced with far more complicated surgery and had been successful with all of them.

'It looks good,' Miles said, coming to stand beside him at the scrub sink.

'Clean,' Will agreed. 'Parapagus twins are the most straightforward when it comes to separation.'

'Should only take somewhere between fifteen to seventeen hours.'

Will nodded, both of them knowing that they'd been in surgery far longer with other conjoined twins over the years. With Ellie and Sarah being conjoined in the lower body, side to side, and given that they didn't share any major veins or arteries, the surgery should indeed be straightforward.

Still, that didn't stop Will from being concerned about Sheena.

'You're frowning,' Miles pointed out. 'What's wrong? Have you found something the rest of us have missed?'

'Do you know what Sheena's planning to do all day while we're in surgery?' He looked back down at his hands, using the special nailbrush to ensure all dirt was definitely gone.

'As far as I know, she's going to fill in at the paediatric clinic and then work on the ward.'

'She's going to work?' Will was instantly concerned.

'She's a fully qualified—and might I add completely brilliant—paediatrician, and as quite a few of her colleagues are here working with us, offering to hold the fort is her way of helping and keeping her mind busy so she doesn't dwell on the girls.'

Will pondered that for a moment then nodded. 'I guess I'd want to keep busy if it were my daughters undergoing extensive surgery.' He elbowed off the taps and turned with his hands held upwards to receive a sterile towel from one of the nurses. He didn't want to be thinking about Sheena at this time, or her well-being, or how she was coping, or anything else for that matter. Of course he was concerned about her, just as he would be about any other parents of conjoined twins, but right now he needed to keep his head in the game. 'Time to be completely focused,' he murmured.

Miles nodded. 'It's never easy operating on

someone you know and love. Those little girls are my goddaughters and I love them very much.'

'There is something special about them,' Will agreed, a small smile tugging at his lips. It had only been a matter of days since he'd met Ellie and Sarah but he knew that both girls had already infiltrated his heart. He'd tried telling himself that they were just another set of conjoined twins, that they were the same as all the other twins he'd operated on over the years, but he knew he was lying to himself.

As he continued to gown and glove, the theatre nurse tying his mask in place, Will looked to where the six-month-old twins had been anaesthetised and were waiting for their surgeons to start this operation.

Soon he stood beside Miles, the two men so in tune with each other that they were able to communicate with simple glances and looks. Right now, both of them seemed to be wearing the same expression, that of complete focus on what was about to happen.

'It's just the same as any other operation,' Will remarked, and Miles nodded.

'Switch off the personal, switch on the professional,' Miles agreed.

They stood there silent for the next minute, waiting for the go-ahead from the anaesthetist. The little girls looked so tiny with tubes and leads coming from them, their radiographs up on the view boxes around the room. On either side of the central theatre were two smaller theatres, which would be used once the girls had been separated.

Paul, the anaesthetist, looked at them and nodded, indicating he was ready. Will looked to Miles. 'For Sheena,' he said softly, and Miles gave an imperceptible nod of agreement.

After addressing the theatre staff, Miles began the slow and careful process of making the first incision. This operation was not about speed, it wasn't about a quick fix. It required a methodical and painstakingly perfect process. No mistakes. Will stood back and watched as his friend and the rest of the team set to work.

When it was time for him to step forward, he

looked again at his friend and could see that Miles was smiling beneath his theatre mask.

'All yours,' Miles remarked, his voice upbeat.

'Thanks. Good to hear that tone in your voice, mate.' The staff shifted around, the orthopaedic theatre nurses coming forward while the others took a much-needed break.

'Let's just say there haven't been any unwanted surprises.'

'That's the type of news I like to hear.' Will checked with the anaesthetist. 'Status?'

The anaesthetist rattled off his statistics before smiling brightly at Will. 'Both Ellie and Sarah are doing remarkably well,' came the jovial reply.

'Excellent.' Will straightened his spine as he looked down at the draped little bodies in front of him, the large conjoined pelvic bone neatly exposed. Separating the girls meant that they would be able to lead normal, healthy, happy lives. Two little dark-haired girls and their dark-haired mother. Three beautiful ladies…all on their own.

Will felt a surge of protectiveness pierce his

heart at this thought but quickly dismissed it. He wasn't a part of Sheena's life any more and yet he'd already come to care deeply for her little girls. He wanted the best for Sarah and Ellie; he wanted to make sure they had every advantage growing up; he wanted them to know how precious they were.

Although he and Miles had told themselves that this surgery was just like any other, that there was nothing different about these babies as opposed to the others they'd operated on, they'd also known that they'd been lying to themselves.

Will paused as he looked down at the girls, a brief moment of panic and fear gripping him. What if something went wrong? What if a problem arose that they'd been unable to anticipate? Would Sheena ever be able to forgive him? The last thing he wanted to do was to cause her pain. After talking with her the other night, he'd come to realise that he was as much at fault for their break-up as Sheena. If only he'd asked her more questions, taken a real interest in *her* rather than simply assuming her life had run a similar course to his own. He'd been blinded by love, blinded by the fact that he'd found his happily-ever-after and had assumed that, because Sheena had admitted her love for him, they would be together for ever.

He'd bought the engagement ring, barely able to contain his excitement at the promise of a rosy future with the woman of his dreams. Then, when she'd turned him down, he'd plummeted, stunned and shocked when she'd confessed she couldn't have children.

For the first time in his life the perfect fairy-tale family picture he'd always had firmly in his mind had started to shake, the foundation of imagination and anticipation nowhere near as solid as he'd thought.

Now, as he was about to perform this intricate surgery on Sheena's beautiful girls, he couldn't help but ponder that if things had gone differently between Sheena and himself, if he'd been less pushy and she'd been more open, these little darlings might have been *his* daughters.

Having always longed to be a father and with those dreams having been cut off with Sheena's rejection, his hopes and dreams had been pushed aside while he'd focused on his career, knowing that medicine was absolute and something he could control. Until he'd met Beatrice, he hadn't realised how much he'd locked his heart away, but being back near Sheena made him realise that what he'd felt for Beatrice paled into insignificance when he was around the mother of these gorgeous twins. She'd allowed him to spend quality time with Sarah and Ellie, and seeing the way they were coming to recognise him when he walked into the room, loving the way they would smile and gurgle and make cute little noises, had unlocked those dreams of parenthood from his heart.

Two little girls—without a father.

Was it possible that if he returned to Australia, if he came home to Adelaide, if he and Sheena could find a basis for a solid friendship, he might be able to fill that void? Surrogate father? It wasn't picture perfect, it wasn't what he'd always dreamed of, but for some reason these two angels had well and truly captured his heart. Even in the short amount of time he'd spent with them during the past few days, watching the way they interacted with Sheena, smiling at the way Sarah always seemed to be the one causing a ruckus while Ellie preferred to keep things calm, Will had been captivated by these twins.

They were different from his other patients because he cared about their mother. That made all the difference in the world. These girls needed him. Sheena needed someone to lean on, someone who knew her well, and with determination coursing through him he decided that he wanted to be that person. First of all, he needed to do what he'd come here to do and focus on this surgery. He'd mentally walked through the operation so many times that it only took a moment to get his thoughts neatly ordered once more.

He raised his gaze to look at the highly skilled staff ready to work with him.

'Let's begin.'

CHAPTER FIVE

WILL was exhausted but elated, and as he stripped off his theatre garb excitement started to grow as he thought about the look on Sheena's face when she saw him heading towards her. She would be tense, nervous, worried. He would smile and she would instantly know that every thing was all right. That her girls were fine.

As he exited Theatres, all ready to give her the good news, he was astounded to discover she wasn't there. He knew she'd planned to work in the paediatric clinic but clinics would be well and truly finished by now. Perhaps she was on the ward. He headed to Paediatrics, still elated at what he and the team of specialists had achieved.

There was always relief when everything had gone according to plan and there was always a strong sense of satisfaction when both babies were doing well after such intense surgery, but this time, with Ellie and Sarah, the two little girls who had completely captured his heart, he felt as though he'd just been handed the moon. Now he could offer that moon to Sheena.

He couldn't hide the smile on his face as he entered the paediatric ward, his gaze eagerly scanning for Sheena. Raquel-Maria and Clementine, at the nurses' station, saw him coming and immediately returned his smile.

'You're out! By the look on your face, it's all good news,' Raquel-Maria commented.

'Yes. Where's Sheena?'

Raquel-Maria shook her head. 'She's not here. She was about an hour ago, but then she left. We thought she'd gone to Theatres to wait.'

Will continued to scan the ward, just in case the women were wrong. 'Try paging her. Calling her. Anything!' Even as he said the words, he was racking his brain to try and figure out where she might have gone. Where would Sheena go? To be alone? To think? To wait?

'She's not answering her phone,' Raquel-Maria said, concern in her tone. 'I wonder where she might be?'

The chapel. The words popped into his head and he remembered the other night, as they'd been walking to catch the taxi to Giuseppe's, she'd mentioned she liked going to the little chapel to think and relax and become one with her thoughts.

'Never mind, Raquel-Maria.' Will headed for the ward door. 'I know where she might be.' He walked briskly along the long corridors, barely able to contain the urge to run through the hospital, desperate to find her, desperate to give her the good news.

Her girls were fine.

He stepped out into the cool October night air and walked across the courtyard to the small brown-brick chapel. She needed to know. Her girls were safe. She needed to know because already half the hospital had received the news and he didn't want the mother to be the last to know.

He pushed open the door with an eagerness that surprised him. He needed to see her, to deliver the news that would bring a smile to her face. He wanted to see that smile, so bright, so wide, causing her eyes to sparkle with happiness.

There were several wooden pews on either side of the aisle, the chapel lit with the glow of large candles, the scent of fresh spring flowers filling the air. There was only one person in the chapel, kneeling down, hands resting on the back of the pew in front, head bowed.

Sheena.

Will rushed down, not caring that he was interrupting her thoughts. 'Sheena!' He didn't speak loudly but it was loud enough for her name to echo softly around the walls. She immediately looked up, seeing him coming towards her, entering the row she was in. She rose to her feet, her face filled with anxiety and pain, her heart pounding with ferocity against her ribs such as she'd never felt before.

Will was here. He must have news about her girls.

'They're fine. They're good. They're better than good.' The words tumbled from his lips, desperate to give her relief from the torment he could see on her face.

'Oh. Oh!' She covered her mouth with one hand as her eyes filled with tears. 'My girls?'

'They're perfect. They handled the surgery with ease. They're strong, those two. Real fighters.' There was great pride in his voice as he spoke. 'There were no complications. Everything went according to plan. Miles and Janessa are monitoring the girls closely in Recovery and everything is perfect. They're *perfect*,' he repeated, his tone conveying his elation.

'Oh, Will. Thank you.' She sniffed and threw her arms about his neck, hugging him close. It was the most natural thing to do, to hold him close as she allowed the emotions of relief and happiness to wash over her. 'Thank you. Thank you. It seems such an insignificant thing to say when I feel so much more, but I can't thank you enough.'

Will's arms automatically slid around her waist, keeping her near. She felt good in his arms. Right. As though she belonged there. As though she'd *always* belonged there. Will pushed the realisation away, knowing he would ponder it in more depth much later. Now that the initial surgery was complete, he might be able to give more thinking time to figuring out what might happen next.

'It's been my pleasure,' he murmured near her ear, content to breathe her in. 'Those girls are fighters. Strong. Independent. Determined. Like their mother.'

'Oh, Will.' Sheena pulled back to look at him. 'That's so…' She swallowed, only realising then just how incredibly close she was to his mouth. His glorious, masterful mouth. Her gaze dipped from his eyes to look at his lips before she met his eyes again. 'Sweet,' she finished on a whisper, and swallowed, the tension and awareness increasing between them until it was so nearly palpable there was nothing left to do but acknowledge it in the only way they knew how.

They stood there, staring at each other for one more second, and Sheena could take it no longer. With her heart filled with thanks, with elation, with hope, she reached up a little higher and urged his head to dip a little lower, causing their mouths to meet.

She thrilled at the instant touch, the light,

feathery sensation as though they were both testing the reaction, both wanting this to happen but also very unsure. There were a lot of what-if's surrounding them and as she stood there, her arms around his neck, her lips brushing once more across his, her breath mingling with his, Sheena shoved all her reservations, all logical thought completely out the door.

This was Will, the man who had not only been instrumental in assuring her girls were safe and healthy but the man who had the ability to set her heart on fire. She wanted this and she could feel it in the way he held her, the way he brushed his mouth over hers, that he wanted it too. Both seemed intrigued to discover whether their experiences over the past ten years had changed anything. The world had always rocked off its axis when they'd been together and with the way he was making her feel now, it appeared that was still the case.

'Sheena,' he murmured against her mouth, kissing her again, unable to believe how incredible this felt.

'Shh,' she whispered. 'It feels so good. Just kiss me, Will.'

He did as she'd bidden, not about to let her down. There had always been a frighteningly natural chemistry existing between them and it was clearly still there, even after a decade of separation. Slowly he allowed his mouth to reacquaint itself with hers, knowing what she liked and what would bring her the most joy.

Holding her close, her body pressed against his, her mouth tilted upwards for his pleasure, he continued to bring them both to the heights, not rushing but giving them both exquisite torture. 'You taste the same. Like always. Sunshine and strawberries.' His tone was thick, husky and filled with desire.

With her breathing erratic from his masterful kisses, Sheena sighed and relaxed against him, the emotions of the past few days starting to subside. 'It was always like this. As though fireworks exploded inside me.' As she rested her head against his chest, her arms slack around his neck, she listened to the thumping of his heart beating beneath his chest. So strong. So vibrant. As it had always been.

'Do you remember our very first kiss?' Will asked a moment later, and Sheena couldn't help but smile.

'I was just thinking about that myself. We'd just finished a gruelling thirty-six-hour shift with that nasty motor vehicle accident.'

'We'd been spending quite a bit of time together.'

'Two Aussies working in London,' she finished. 'I was tired and on my way back to my accommodation and you insisted on walking with me.'

'It was three o'clock in the morning, Sheena,' he protested. 'I wanted to make sure you were safe.'

'You walked me to my door at the old nurses' home and we stood on the step, in the cold, staring at each other.'

Will eased back and looked down at her. 'You looked so tired and exhausted but I could tell you were excited, I could see it in your eyes.'

Sheena smiled up at him, her arms still about

his neck as they both took a trip down memory lane. 'You shuffled your feet, you put your hands into your pockets and you tried not to stare at my lips.'

'You had the most gorgeous mouth…you still do.'

Sheena felt a thrill of delight buzz through her at his words, amazed that after so long apart the deep-seated need for him was still very much alive.

'I wasn't sure whether you'd let me kiss you or deck me one.'

'I was hoping you'd give in to the thing that was between us—it was so electric, wasn't it?'

'You hesitated with your key. You didn't put it straight into the lock and go inside. You stopped and looked at me and you didn't seem to want to head in.'

'I didn't. I wanted you to kiss me.'

'And I did.'

Sheena sighed. 'And it was the most perfect kiss I've ever experienced.'

'Really?' Will smiled, trying not to preen like a peacock at this news.

'Yes…although this kiss wasn't so bad either.'

'Wasn't so bad?' He smiled down at her and her heart melted. 'I think I'm going to ignore that but only because we need to go and see your girls.'

Sheena breathed in deeply and slowly eased out of his arms. 'Yes. My babies.' She nodded, although Will could sense a hint of hesitancy in her words.

'Is something wrong?'

'What?' She looked at him in the dim light of the church. 'No. Nothing's wrong.' She smiled and nodded. 'Let's go and see them.'

'Right.' He stepped back so they could exit from the seats and as they walked down the aisle of the small, quiet chapel, he could sense the excited anticipation radiating from her. She'd been through so much, especially today, and finally she had the opportunity to go and see her daughters after their life-changing surgery.

As they walked through the hospital, it was apparent that the good news had travelled fast and everyone they met seemed to beam brightly with happiness at the news that the girls were doing well.

'Fantastic news, Sheena,' one nurse said as they passed in the corridor.

'So happy for the babies,' a cleaner said as they rounded a corner.

Will was happy to share in Sheena's elation as she received comments from her co-workers but what surprised him was the level of elation coursing through him. It was odd simply because he'd performed far more difficult separation surgery, which had dragged on for far longer than today's operation, and still hadn't felt this level of happiness. Why was he so happy? So upbeat?

He glanced at the woman walking beside him, the woman who was smiling so brightly he knew her cheek muscles must be hurting. She looked so incredibly beautiful with her eyes sparkling and her cheeks all rosy. He swallowed and licked his lips, surprised to find the taste of Sheena still lingering there.

It was then he realised it wasn't just the successful operation that had him so happy but the fact that he'd kissed Sheena. It was something he'd promised himself he wouldn't do, but how was he to know that the attraction he'd felt for this woman had only been lying dormant, waiting to be reawakened with her sweet laugh, her sunny smiles and her alluring scent?

'There you are,' the theatre sister remarked as they headed into the theatre block. 'Janessa and Miles have been expecting you.'

'Sorry.' Sheena clasped her hands together as she walked along the corridors and more people offered their happy thoughts at the joyous outcome for the girls. All of it—the sights, the sounds, the smells—became muted. All she could hear as she advanced towards the theatres where the girls were being monitored was the sound of her pounding heart.

Her girls, her beautiful babies, had been separated. They were both alive and progressing well. It was the news she'd only prayed she'd hear, but now that the moment of actually seeing them was upon her, she was gripped with fear. Not fear for her girls but rather fear for the enormous task ahead of her.

Was she up to the task of being both mother and father to her twins? Up until now she hadn't been able to focus on anything else except the surgery. Now that it was over, she felt as though she had the weight of the world on her shoulders. Her feet started to drag and she licked her suddenly dry lips, her eyes wide with concern.

'Sheena?' Will stopped and waited for her when he realised she'd slowed down. 'What's wrong?' he asked, the smile sliding from his face as he watched her closely.

She stopped, swallowed and tried again, feeling silly for voicing her fears out loud. 'I'm…I'm scared, Will.'

'Scared? What about? The girls are strong, they're fighters and they're fine. They're both healthy. Of course, they'll each require further surgery but that's all minor and quite a few weeks away. For now, though, everything is looking better than expected, better than the surgical teams could have hoped.'

'I know. I know, and I appreciate everyone's efforts, their skills, their support, their caring, but…now it's all up to me.'

Panic was beginning to rise in her voice and anxiety was written all over her face. 'In six months,' she said, 'Miles and Janessa will head off overseas, doing their own thing, helping others, and that's good. I'm really happy for them. Everyone else here at the hospital has their own lives despite how much they care for my girls. I'll leave the hospital and I'll be all alone. I have nowhere to take my girls when we leave here and wherever we end up, I'll be raising them on my own and what if—?'

Will leaned forward and placed a finger across her lips to stop her talking. He *had* thought of kissing her to shut her up. It was what he would have done in years gone by and although they'd just shared a few kisses, he had no idea what any of it meant. Had she simply been grateful for what he'd done for her girls? Had she been overcome with relief? Had she used her situation as an excuse to be close to him and, if so, why? What did she want from him? Right now, though, he could see she was confused and anxious about her girls, about her life, her future.

Calming her down was the first step to figuring out what was really going on.

'What if you're fine? You, the girls—all fine. This is the next stage, Sheena. The next chapter.' His tone was calm but firm and he held her gaze, watching as her panic slowly subsided as his words wound themselves around her. 'You've been in survival mode since the girls were born, probably even before that with your husband leaving you in the lurch.' The protective urge he felt towards Sheena came to the fore again and he had to quickly hold it at bay.

'Everything over the past six months has been building towards this day, this hour, this second. That's quite intense. All of your energies have been focused on coping with feeding, bathing, changing and sleeping. They're your girls, Sheena. The babies you thought you'd never have, and for the first time in their lives your girls are currently in separate cribs. *Separate!* That's huge.' He placed his hands on her shoulders and looked down into her eyes, intent on helping her through this.

'It's only natural to have questions, to be worried and concerned, but you can't let that scare you. You're stronger than that. Let's go and see them. Soon you'll be able to hold them. You'll be able to smother them with kisses, to bath them, to dress them in clothes that don't need to be specially made. You've given them the chance to lead normal, healthy lives and that's the one thing every mother wants for her children. You'll be able to cuddle them, one at a time. Or you could have Ellie in one arm and Sarah in the other. And if that gets too much or your arms get too sore, call me. I'm eager to have a cuddle with each of those gorgeous girls. You hold one. I'll hold the other.'

Sheena couldn't help but smile at his words. She sighed, feeling calmer, more in control, better able to cope, and it was all thanks to Will. Not only had he assisted with the intense surgical procedure which had separated her girls, he'd put her mind to rest against the fear and trepidation that had been slowly building throughout the past six months and had only just hit her— square in the face—throughout this day.

'It's just like you to know exactly what to say

to make me feel better. Thank you, Will.' His words had given her courage and hope. 'I know it's not going to be easy. I know I'm going to need support and help, and as I'm not very good at asking for either, I guess I'll have to learn.'

Will agreed and dropped his hands back to his sides, pleased he'd been able to help out. He'd also been serious when he'd suggested she call him if she needed help. 'Just take things one step at a time. For now you're surrounded by people who care for you, Sheena. Once you leave the hospital, don't forget there are a lot of community support services as well. You won't be on your own.'

Excitement started to replace fear and she couldn't contain it as her eyes flashed with delight. 'I *do* want to see them.' Love filled her heart. 'I'm *desperate* to see them, and you're so right, Will. This is the next chapter of my life. It's not going to be an easy road but I'll do it. I have to face my fears sometime, right?'

'That's the Sheena I know.' He winked at her as she once more started to walk, eager now to see her daughters. She was facing her fears with her head held high and he was incredibly proud of her for that…which only made her even more difficult to resist.

When he ushered her into Recovery she stood there, looking at her daughters, who were, for the very first time, sleeping in separate cribs. Janessa and Miles, along with several other specialists, were attending the babies, but when Sheena entered the room they stepped back, smiles on their tired faces as she walked slowly towards her girls.

'Thank you,' she murmured to the room in general, the words heartfelt and filled with sincerity, but her gaze was solely trained on her babies. She shook her head as though she couldn't quite believe it. 'They're separated.' The words were whispered, catching against the emotion choking her throat, but in the quiet of the room, everyone heard.

She reached out to Ellie, tenderly brushing her fingers across the baby's face before leaning down and kissing her daughter. Then she turned and walked over to where the other crib was situated and did the same thing to Sarah, a gentle caress and then the kiss of a mother who loved her babies very much.

From his vantage point in the doorway, Will watched the entire scene and when he felt his own throat start to thicken, he looked around the room, watching as other people followed Sheena's actions, all of them almost as happy as the mother herself that everything had gone according to plan, with no surprises during the surgery and no complications thus far.

Sheena reluctantly tore her gaze away from her beloved babies to look at everyone in the room—the nurses, the doctors, the surgeons, some, like Janessa, who were lifelong friends, and others, like Marta, who she'd only met the day before.

'Thank you. Thank you all so much.' She clutched her hands to her chest, her words sincere.

Then she looked over at Will and while the look of appreciation and thanks was still definitely in her eyes, they seemed to soften as they rested on him. 'I still can't believe this has really happened.' She swallowed, her tongue flicking out to wet her dry lips, and Will felt a tightening in his gut. Her lips. Her gorgeous, succulent, perfectly plump lips. Lips that not ten minutes ago had been pressed to his.

'It's good to see,' Miles remarked, coming to stand beside Will as Sheena fussed over her two girls. 'A mother who is so in love with her daughters.'

'It's very good.' Will continued to watch Sheena's every move, as though unable to look away from the mesmerising sight. She was so at home with her girls and even though she'd confessed her doubts, he knew they were all for naught. Anyone seeing her with Sarah and Ellie would think the same.

'It's not going to be easy—the road ahead. She's going to need a lot of help,' Miles remarked.

'Agreed, but she's a natural mother with a healthy dose of common sense. She'll be terrific,' Will added.

'Especially if she has help. From people she trusts. People she's known for a long time,' Miles said. 'People like Janessa and myself…and you.'

'What are you trying to imply, Miles?' Will asked, tearing his gaze away from Sheena to look at his friend with a hint of impatience.

'You're someone she trusts, Will.'

'And?'

'And you're due to return to Philly in about five weeks' time.'

'Yeah. So?'

'So…what happens after that? What do you really have waiting for you back in the States? Beatrice didn't exactly take your broken engagement quietly and as she's now a permanent hospital lawyer, it can't make life all that enjoyable for you.'

'What are you getting at, Miles?'

'Why don't you return to South Australia? Your parents are here. Some of your siblings are here.' He paused and said more quietly, 'The people you really care about are all here. So what's keeping you in the States? Think about it.' Miles slapped his friend on the back before returning to his duties.

Will pondered his friend's words. He couldn't deny he'd given some thought to how his life might change if he moved back to Australia permanently. Sorting out his past with Sheena had helped free up a lot of mind space. It had also made him realise why things had felt wrong with Beatrice. He knew he could have cut back his hours at the hospital when Beatrice had asked him to, if he'd really wanted to, but he could now admit that that hadn't been what he'd wanted.

If he came back to Australia he would definitely cut back on the hours he worked, especially if it meant he could spend more time with Sheena and the twins. It was no secret that those little girls had stolen his heart and he knew he'd do anything for them.

He'd been planning a life with Beatrice and he knew that had they had children, he would have been a hands-on father. Still, he wouldn't have made the work sacrifice *just* for Beatrice. He thought about Sheena, about if they were together and if *she* had been the one to ask him to cut back his hours. Would he have done it?

He frowned a little as he realised the answer. It was yes.

CHAPTER SIX

TWENTY-FOUR hours later, Will went to see how Sheena and the girls were coping. The twins had been in induced comas in order to help them heal and recover. He knew the head anaesthetist, Paul, had been around to review them, and from what Will had just read in Ellie's chart, it looked as though she was doing a little better than Sarah.

He'd only left the hospital once, to return to his parents' house where he was staying, for a quick shower and change of clothes, before coming back to monitor his small patients. He knew he should try to get more sleep but the simple fact of the matter was that he was worried about not only Ellie and Sarah but Sheena as well.

She was sitting in a comfortable chair opposite where her daughters slept, their individual cribs pushed as close as possible. Will stood there, watching her sleep, unable to believe how peaceful she looked. She deserved some peace, some support, some help. He knew she was overwhelmed by the huge job before her but he knew of old that she had so much inner strength she'd do fine…but she'd still be alone.

'Hey,' Miles said softly behind him, and Will turned, unaware his friend had even come into the room. 'How are the girls?'

'Vitals are all good. Sarah's running a bit of a temperature, but it's being closely monitored.' Will angled his head towards the door and both men exited, eager to allow Sheena to sleep for as long as possible. 'Sheena's exhausted,' Will told his friend as they headed towards Miles's small office situated off to the side of the paediatric ward.

'How do you think she's really doing?' Miles asked as the two men sat down.

Will thought carefully before answering. 'She's had a lot to cope with but I think sleeping will help her the most at the moment, allow her body and mind to relax.'

'And how are *you* doing?'

'Me?' Will gave his friend a quizzical glance. 'I'm fine. The operation was a complete success so it looks as though those two little girls can live out very normal, very healthy lives with their mother.'

'I was referring to you seeing Sheena again. It appears you've both managed to work through whatever happened all those years ago.'

'Yes.' Will stood and shoved his hands into his trouser pockets. 'It's all behind us.'

'And you don't think there's any way the two of you can…reconcile?'

'Trying to play matchmaker, Miles?'

'You and Sheena were good together all those years ago. I remember. Now when I see you two together again it just seems…oh, I don't know… right somehow. Janessa and I think the four of you would make a great family.'

'No.' Will immediately shook his head. 'While there might still be some remnant of attraction between Sheena and myself, it doesn't mean there's a future as a family.'

'But you want a family. You've always wanted a family.'

'But this family doesn't belong to me. Those girls—'

'Have no father.'

'That doesn't mean it's up to me to fill the position.' Will paced angrily around Miles's office, back and forth in the small space. 'I've always wanted *my* family. To father my own children. I don't even know if Sheena can *have* more children.'

'There's a slim chance she can,' Miles informed him. 'Her gynaecologist is waiting until she's finished breastfeeding the girls before he makes any decisions, but as far as I've been told, her endometriosis is still bad. It's not as bad as it used to be but as far as I know, she may need to have further surgery, possibly an oophorectomy.'

Will was stunned. 'Why didn't anyone tell me? Why didn't Sheena tell me?'

Miles shrugged. 'She's a strong woman, Will. She's been used to coping with big decisions on her own for quite some time now and she'll keep on coping. Unless she has someone she can lean on…now and then.'

Will frowned, pondering his friend's words. If

Sheena needed another operation, if she had an oophorectomy, then she would never be able to have any more children. Ellie and Sarah would be all she'd have and it made those little girls even more precious.

'When did everything become so difficult?' he remarked, shoving his fingers through his hair. 'Ever since I was little, I just wanted to grow up, become a doctor, meet a nice woman, get married, have children and live happily ever after.'

'I know what you mean. That's how I always thought my life would pan out and I thought it had, before my first wife died.' Miles nodded solemnly. 'It's not about where we think we'll end up but how we get there. Janessa's shown me that. She's lost so much in her life and yet those losses have only made her stronger. Sheena's the same. Nessa says that's why the two of them are such close friends, because they've both been to that dark place where they have to endure a lot in order to fight their way out.'

Miles met Will's gaze fair and square. 'You deserve happiness, Will. So does Sheena. She's a woman of substance and she'll deal with whatever comes her way and she'll do it on her own if she has to and I have no doubt that she'll do a bang-up job, but wouldn't it be great if she didn't have to? Wouldn't it be great if she had someone who loved those little girls as much as she did to help her raise them?'

'The twins have a father. He should be here, raising them, supporting Sheena.'

'But he isn't. He's a self-centred, egotistical pig who kicked his pregnant wife out of her home and then divorced her for breach of contract.' Miles gritted his teeth. 'Life isn't fair and Sheena knows that.'

'She really is going to keep soldiering on, isn't she?' Will stated rhetorically. 'Whether I'm in her life or not, she'll move forward, she'll raise those girls on her own, even though she's incredibly scared.'

Realising that Sheena would do what needed to be done, would continue, without any support if necessary, to raise her girls, had helped to dispel the picture of the perfect fairy-tale family he'd always carried within his heart.

Life wasn't fair. Things hadn't worked out between Sheena and himself all those years ago. Was it possible that he really was being given a second chance? Ellie and Sarah weren't biologically his daughters but they still needed a father.

Will spun on his heel and headed out of Miles's office, back towards the girls' private room. He stopped outside the door and looked in through the small window at Sheena. Although there were blinds on the window, he could see between the slats. She still sat in the chair, laptop on her knee as she stared at something on the screen. Shifting slightly, Will could see she was studying the various radiographs of her daughters as though she still couldn't believe they were now separated.

He could tell, just by looking at the slight slump of her shoulders and the way her head seemed too heavy to hold upright, that she was exhausted but he also knew her stubbornness of old. She wouldn't sleep, at least not properly, until she was certain that both her girls were out of danger. Being a trained paediatrician, she knew that the first twenty-four hours were critical and that monitoring the babies was of utmost importance.

Walking quietly into the room, he glanced at Sheena and saw that although the laptop was on her lap, her eyes were closed. He headed over to the cribs and smiled down at Ellie, sleeping all on her own, with no Sarah to accidentally kick her awake. He was pleased Sheena had insisted the cribs be pushed as close together as possible as research had shown that once conjoined twins were separated, they could often suffer feelings of abandonment. After all, for their entire existence they'd always had someone else right there beside them. He brushed his finger across Ellie's cheek and smiled. She was gorgeous, adorable and so like her mother.

He looked at the machines that were giving readouts of oxygen saturations, EEG and fluid intake and output. He unhooked his stethoscope and placed it over Ellie's chest, listening to her heart rate, confirming it against the EEG. Pleased with her progress, he shuffled around to check on Sarah, frowning a little at the differing readouts. The fluid intake and output wasn't as steady as Ellie's and Sarah's heart was beating at a slightly higher rate. He checked it with his stethoscope, confirming the readings from the machine, and ensured the oxygen non-rebreather mask, which was over her mouth and nose, was securely in place.

'How's she doing?'

Will quickly turned to look at Sheena, sitting in the chair, unsure, in the dim light, whether her eyes were open or closed.

'She's stabilising so that's good.'

'I didn't hear you come in.'

A small smile tugged at his lips. 'Good, because I was trying not to wake you. Have you managed to get much sleep?'

'No, but, then, I'm used to it,' she said on a sigh. Shifting slowly, as though her muscles were a little stiff, she placed the laptop on the table beside her and stood. She wiggled her shoulders and turned her head from side to side before putting her arms up above her head and stretching. 'I was just thinking earlier that I should set up the small camp bed and lie down properly, rather than dozing on and off in the chair.' She smothered a yawn. 'I think the dozing makes me more tired.'

'I think the lack of sleep and high stress levels are what's causing your exhaustion,' he returned, but Sheena could hear the caring note in his words. Will still cared for her and where she'd initially thought it was only because she was the mother of his patients, after the kiss they'd shared in the small chapel, she was desperate to believe it was due to their shared past.

'You have a point. What about you? Have you managed some sleep? That was one gruelling operation you all performed yesterday.'

'I've grabbed a few hours here and there. During the surgery we were working in teams with planned breaks so none of us became exhausted.'

'And I appreciate that. Honestly, Will, saying just a simple "Thank you" to everyone feels so… inadequate.' She walked over to Ellie's crib and looked down at her little girl. 'My babies are no longer conjoined and while I understand the medical side of the surgery and appreciate everyone's skill, the fact of the matter is that my daughters are now able to grow up and lead a more normal life. That's huge.'

Will hooked his stethoscope back around his neck and shifted to stand at the base of both cribs. 'It's what every mother wants for their children. A normal, happy life.'

'Yes.' She rested a hand on Ellie's head, her thumb moving back and forth, caressing her child, who was sleeping peacefully. 'I know there are still long days ahead, especially with Sarah.' She swallowed painfully. 'You know, I never thought I'd be one of those mothers who panicked and fretted over their children. I'm a trained paediatrician. I've seen so many different things happen to children and I have the knowledge and medical expertise to be able to help others. Now, though, I look at these two and realise that I could hold every medical degree in the world and still not have a clue what to do if both of them are screaming and crying at the same time.' She forced a laugh but he could hear fear and uncertainty in her words.

'You're borrowing trouble, Sheena. It's probably one of your biggest weaknesses. You overthink and then you panic and, while you're internally strong and can accomplish anything you put your mind to, you have to let go of all the questions that surround your future. Believe me when I say that you're going to be fine.'

'Do you really think so?'

Will crossed to her side and looked down into her face. 'I know so, Sheena. You're…amazing!'

Sheena's heart started to beat wildly against her chest at his words. 'Really?'

'I would never lie to you.'

Sheena wasn't sure what to think, what to say. He was standing close, so close she could breathe him in, the kisses they'd shared in the chapel coming instantly to mind. Her gaze momentarily dipped to his lips and she was about to ask him about the kisses they'd shared when a small cry, more like a hiccup, came from Ellie. Sheena immediately returned her attention to her daughter. And there in her crib, amongst all the tubes and monitoring paraphernalia, Ellie opened her eyes for the first time since surgery, and looked at her mother.

'Oh. Oh, Will. Look. She's awake!'

Will looked down at beautiful little Ellie, and the baby gave them a sleepy smile.

Love, pure and simple, flowed through Sheena as she bent and kissed her daughter. 'Oh, it's so magnificent, so perfect. Oh, Ellie, honey. Mummy was so worried about you.'

'Yes,' Will agreed, unable, in his elation at seeing Ellie awake, to resist dropping his arm around Sheena's shoulders. 'I think you're going to do much better than *fine*.'

'I need to hold her, Will. I need to hold her.'

'Let's make that happen,' he said, and together they wheeled all the machines that were attached to Ellie over towards the comfortable chair and within a few minutes Will had lifted Ellie from the crib and placed her, for the first time, in her mother's arms.

'Oh, my sweet Ellie. My gorgeous girl.' Sheena held her close and Will couldn't help but kneel down beside the chair, slipping his arm back around Sheena's shoulders, elated when she leaned over and put her head on his shoulder, the two of them staring down at the still sleepy baby.

'This is one of the most precious moments of my life,' Sheena whispered. She lifted her head and turned to look at Will. 'I'm so happy you were here to share it with me.'

Will nodded. 'I'm honoured.' And it was the most natural thing in the world to lean closer and press a kiss to her lips.

It was another twenty-four hours before Sarah decided to settle down, to stop scaring her mother by indulging in high temperatures, and opened her eyes.

Sheena's heart instantly lifted when she saw her daughter's wide blue eyes looking up at her from the crib. 'You're all right. My beautiful Sarah.' Sheena kissed her daughter who, now that she was awake, was already making herself known.

'She's going to give you lots of grey hairs when she's older,' Janessa remarked. Her friend was seated in the comfortable chair, giving Ellie a bottle.

'With the way she peaked a high temperature, I'd say she's already started,' Sheena countered, desperate to pick Sarah up but knowing it was difficult with the tubes and drains still attached to the baby. She pressed the buzzer, letting the staff at the nurses' desk know she needed some help, but as Sarah was starting to work herself up into a real frenzy, Sheena bent over the crib and brushed kisses onto Sarah's cheek. The baby girl tried to hold out her arms to her mother but couldn't because of the drips, which only caused her crying volume to increase.

'Shh. Shh. Mummy's here. Mummy's here,' Sheena crooned. 'It's all right. I'm here.' Thankfully, Sarah started to respond to her mother's voice and when Raquel-Maria came in, Sheena smiled. 'Sorry to disturb you from your duties,' she said to the nurse.

'Sarah's woken up?' Raquel-Maria's smile was wide and filled with delight. 'Well, of course I can *hear* that she's awake. Oh, how wonderful. That's just wonderful. I take it you want to feed her? Right, then. Let's get you settled.'

A few minutes later Sheena was seated in another comfortable chair, silence filling the air as Sarah greedily suckled at her breast. It was incredible to be able to hold her children one at a time and to feed them, rather than having to constantly express milk. 'Oh, baby. Slow down,' she crooned, settling Sarah a bit better. 'The last thing you need right now is a tummyache.'

'Too true,' Janessa remarked. 'Look, Sheenie. Ellie's fallen back to sleep with just the last bit of her bottle left, but when I try to take it from her mouth, she starts madly sucking again.'

'I know. She often does that. It's so cute.' Sheena sighed and looked across at her other daughter. 'They're both going to be fine. Sarah's awake now and they're both going to be fine.' There was determination in Sheena's tone, mixed with a healthy dose of relief.

'Yes, they are,' Janessa agreed. 'Both Miles and Will are extremely happy with their progress and no doubt Raquel-Maria is off phoning them to let them both know that Sarah's awake.' Janessa looked at the clock on the wall. 'I give Will…under ten minutes before he gets here.'

'He won't just drop everything and race here.'

'Why not? Technically, the girls are his only patients, although now that the major surgery is over, I have to tell you that Charisma is looking to headhunt Will for the hospital.'

'Really?' Sheena looked away, focusing her attention back on Sarah as she tried to process this news. If Will stayed, that would mean he would be here in Adelaide longer than his currently scheduled two months. Could it be possible that they could be granted more time together to figure out what on earth was happening between them? Was the attraction they still felt only residual? Would it stand the test of time? Would she be able to open up to him completely, tell him her deepest, innermost thoughts and secrets? She didn't know but having more time definitely increased the odds.

'H-how long do you think Charisma wants him to work here?' She tried to make her words sound as though she were asking the question about any other member of staff, as though Will working here at Adelaide Mercy was really nothing special.

'Stop trying to be so casual about it.' Janessa saw through her bluff neatly. 'I know you far too well. Of course you want Will to stay.'

'What makes you say that?'

'I've seen the way the two of you look at each other.'

Surprised that they'd been so closely observed, Sheena raised her eyebrows. 'What way?'

Janessa smiled. 'The way Miles and I look at each other.'

Sheena shook her head. 'No. Will does not look at me the way Miles looks at you. Miles worships the ground you walk on. He would get you the moon if you asked him to.' She shook her head again. 'Will doesn't look at me like that.'

'Oh, no? Then why was it that I almost walked in on the two of you kissing yesterday?'

'What?' Sheena's throat went instantly dry and her cheeks tinged with pink as heat washed over her. 'You…'

'I came to check on the girls and opened the door—saw you sitting in this chair, holding Ellie, Will kneeling beside you, locking his lips to yours.' Janessa's smile was very bright. 'So?' Excitement filled her friend's voice.

'So?' Sheena replied.

'So…what does it mean?' Janessa blurted. 'Are the two of you back together? The old feelings have come to the surface once again and if Will stays here in Adelaide, you'll be able to—'

'Whoa! Whoa, there.' Sheena held up her free hand. 'For a start, Will and I are not back together. He kissed me quickly on my lips because we were caught up in the moment. That's all. Nothing romantic about it. Ellie had just woken up and it was…' She shrugged as she searched for the right words to describe how she'd felt. 'I don't know…it was…it just felt right. Like a celebratory kiss.' There was no way she was telling Janessa about the kisses she and Will had shared in the chapel.

'Are you trying to tell me that you're not well on your way to falling in love with Will all over again?'

Sheena swallowed. 'No. I'm not saying that at all. I'm saying that I'm confused and emotional and…I rejected him, Janessa.' She shook her head as though that one strike against her could never be fully removed. 'I refused his marriage proposal. It doesn't matter whether we've cleared the air or not, no man is going to come back for more when he's already been rejected.'

'But Will is no ordinary man, Sheena. From what I've seen, he's not the sort of man to let a past mistake stand in the way of true happiness.'

Sheena absorbed Janessa's words, hope starting to rise. 'Do you really think so?'

'I do. Now, tell me straight. Do you still have feelings for him?' Janessa persisted.

Sheena looked away, then back to her sister, knowing she couldn't lie. 'Yes. Of course. We had a past. I keep remembering the good times we shared and all the things we wanted to do. We were happy. I want that happiness again.'

'Good. Admitting it is the first step. Uh…' Janessa thought of another question. 'Do you want these feelings to continue to grow?'

'Yes, but—'

'Ah. No buts. Do you want Will to reciprocate these feelings?'

'Well, of course I do but I hurt him—'

'Shh.' Janessa cut her off. 'Let it go. Let the past and the hurt and the rejection and everything that went along with it…go. That's the first step in gluing this relationship back together.'

'Nessa, it's not that simple. I have the girls to think about now. I can't put my needs and desires before theirs. They need me and I need them. I don't have time for any sort of romance. I'm a mother first and foremost and unlike my own mother, who didn't give me the time of day, I intend to be there for Ellie and Sarah, to let them know without a doubt that they are truly loved. There's simply no time now for romance.'

As she finished talking, Will walked into the room and Sheena's heart instantly jumped with delight. Her mouth lifted in a smile and her eyes sparkled with happiness.

'Right,' Janessa said softly, not believing her friend for a moment. She glanced pointedly at the clock. 'Eight and a half minutes. Not bad.'

'Quiet,' Sheena said, but turned and smiled at Will. 'Hi.' She couldn't help the way her heart thrummed with delight the instant he appeared, the way her breath caught in her throat at the sight of him and the way she could feel a blush suffuse her cheeks at being noticed by him. Thank goodness she was already sitting down because with the demanding and protective way he'd entered her room, like a knight coming to rescue his princess, Sheena knew her knees wouldn't have been able to support her. Was Janessa right? Was Will still interested in her? Sheena could only hope. The fact that he had indeed come to the room less than ten minutes after Raquel-Maria had left to notify him surely meant something? Right?

Of course, given that he was such a brilliant doctor, he would be concerned about his patients, but Sheena wanted to believe it was more than that. After the moments they'd shared yesterday when Ellie had initially woken up after the long, life-changing surgery, Will had been so pleased that he'd been there to witness it. He'd been as excited as Sheena that Ellie was doing so well. Was he like this with all his patients and their parents, or was it just her? Was she special to him?

Twice Will had kissed her. Twice she had responded. Were they really moving towards some sort of reconciliation and they hadn't even realised? Was he able to forgive her for turning him down all those years ago? It seemed so and if things did progress, if they *were* able to rekindle their relationship, would he be able to accept Ellie and Sarah as his own? Sheena watched him as he immediately came to her side and knelt down beside the chair, hope filling her heart.

'I was told Sarah had woken up. That's excellent news. I only wish I'd been here for it, as I was with Ellie.'

'I'll bet,' Janessa murmured beneath her breath, a secret smile on her lips.

Sheena ignored Janessa and looked from Sarah, who was sleeping contentedly in her arms, to Will…his face so close to hers. 'Yes. My darling Sarah opened her eyes, dragged in a deep breath and screamed until she was fed.' Sheena told him.

Will's deep, rich chuckle was her answer. 'I can well believe it.' Tenderly he stroked the baby's head. 'Hello, Sarah,' he whispered. 'Good to have you back with us.' Sheena watched Will closely, a lump in her throat at the way he seemed to adore her girls. Their heads were almost touching as he bent and placed a kiss on Sarah forehead. 'So small. So precious. So special.'

'Yes.'

When he looked at her, the rest of the world seemed to melt away and all that was left was the two of them and the girls. The possibility of a family. Her heart was linked with his, pounding in unison to the same rhythm.

With the increase in her breathing rate due to his nearness, due to the way his gaze seemed to bore into hers with repressed need and desire, Sheena parted her lips to allow the pent-up air to escape. Her tongue slipped out to wet her dry lips and she swallowed, wondering if she was imagining the way Will's mouth seemed to be drawing closer to her own.

Was he going to kiss her again? Was it that he was happy that Sarah was awake or was it something else? Was this really happening? Confusion continued to war with barely veiled passion that seemed to burn through her whenever he was this close.

'Sheenie,' he whispered, his breath fanning out to warm her, to caress her, to lure her closer.

Almost…almost…

Beep, beep, beep.

'Blast!' Janessa murmured, digging in her pocket to switch off her pager at the same time that Will instantly straightened, putting distance between himself and Sheena. The outside world returned with a bang. Will stood and straightened his tie before shoving his hands into his pockets.

'Sorry. Don't mind me,' Janessa said.

Sheena could quite clearly see the look on her friend's face, the one where she was trying not to grin too widely at the 'almost kiss' she'd witnessed.

'It's the unit,' Janessa remarked after looking at her pager. 'Sorry, but I need to go. Will, can you help me put Ellie back into her crib, please? Then I'll leave you to help Sheena.'

'Of course.' Will carefully worked with Janessa to wheel the machines connected to Ellie back towards the crib, and after Janessa laid the baby on the soft mattress he quickly checked

Ellie's vitals, ensuring the machines were working correctly.

'Now that Sarah's awake,' Janessa continued, brushing her finger over Ellie's cheek, 'Charisma will no doubt schedule the press conference for first thing in the morning. You can give your prepared statement, have your photograph taken with the girls and then hopefully the media will leave you in peace.'

Sheena groaned. 'The press conference. I'd forgotten about that.'

'Well, I'm needed in the NICU, so I'll leave the two of you to discuss the ins and outs of PR… and anything else that might come to mind.' Janessa winked at them before heading to the door. Soon Sheena and her girls were alone with Will once more.

'Do I really have to do the silly photo shoot?'

Will nodded. 'PR helps with the hospital budget,' he pointed out, but jerked his thumb towards the door. 'What's with Janessa? She was acting a little strange, don't you think?'

'Janessa saw you kiss me yesterday.' As well as witnessing the 'almost kiss' they'd just shared, she wanted to add, but as Will hadn't actually kissed her, she didn't want him to think she was jumping to conclusions.

'Ah.' Dawning realisation crossed his face and he shoved his hands into his trouser pockets again. 'That would explain it.' He paused as though completely uncertain what to say next. He looked at her, she looked at him and the rest of the world seemed to disappear. It was how it had always been when they were alone together. Sheena could sense the tension increasing between them and when Will held her gaze for a moment, the increase in her breathing rate was automatic.

'We were good together,' he murmured, still standing beside Ellie's crib as though he needed to keep some distance between them.

Sheena nodded. 'Always. We were friends first, though.'

'We were,' he agreed.

'Do you think…?' She paused and swallowed. 'I mean, is it possible for us to become close friends again?'

Will shook his head and closed his eyes for a

moment before meeting her gaze once more. 'I want to be friends, Sheena. I've really missed just being with you, talking to you. We share the same sense of humour, the same outlook on things. I think, after you left, that's what really hit me the most. That my friend was gone…gone from my life.'

'I'm here now,' she offered quietly. 'Perhaps reconnecting through the girls is our second chance to rekindle our friendship.'

He nodded. 'Perhaps it is.' Friendship was a good place to start but he had to confess that sharing in her quiet moments with Ellie and Sarah, feeling the joy and elation pass through her as she held her girls, made him want more than just friendship. Deep down inside, he admitted he wanted to be a part of her life. He wanted to help her make decisions, to spend more time with the girls, not only in a medical capacity but as an important person in their lives.

Sarah shifted a little in Sheena's arms and Will smiled.

'Is Sarah getting too heavy?'

'I think it's time to put her back in her crib.' Sheena looked down at her baby and smiled. 'It's so wonderful to be able to hold both of them individually. So…' She searched for the right word.

'Heart-warming?' Will suggested.

'Exactly. See? We're still very much in tune with each other. Friendship is a good place to start.'

Will came over and together they settled the still sleeping baby into her crib and again Will checked the machines to ensure they were working correctly and performed Sarah's observations, pleased with the outcome.

'She's definitely over that fever,' he said, bending down to kiss Sarah's head. 'Clever girl.' He turned and looked at Sheena, who was trying to smother a yawn.

'Let's get this small camp bed set up for you so you can get some proper rest, rather than just napping in the chair.'

Sheena nodded, talking as they set up the bed. 'Now that Sarah's woken up from the induced coma and they've both been fed and changed, exhaustion seems to be swamping me at every turn.'

Will smiled. 'It's to be expected. You've been through so much, Sheenie.' He turned down the covers for her and waited while she slipped off her shoes and lay down, her hand covering her mouth as she yawned yet again.

'Your girls are fine,' he murmured as he knelt beside her and pulled the covers up, gently tucking her in.

Sheena yawned, wanting to talk to him some more, wanting to thank him for everything he'd done, but her eyes refused to stay open one second more.

Her breathing instantly settled and he knew she was asleep. Tenderly, his fingers swept her hair back from her forehead and his gut tightened as he looked down at this sleeping beauty. Bending down, he brushed a kiss across her lips. 'Sleep sweet, Sheena,' he murmured, before walking to the chair and sitting down. He intended to stay here, to monitor the babies and give Sheena the opportunity to have a proper sleep. As the three of them slept soundly, Will nodded. Relaxing back into the chair, he felt a sense of contentment he hadn't felt in well over a decade. It felt right to be here. With Sheena. With the twins. It felt right to be watching over them.

'Three beautiful girls,' he whispered into the quiet room, then smiled.

CHAPTER SEVEN

For the next few days Will spent quite a bit of time with Sheena and the twins, pleased that Sheena was allowing him the opportunity to really get to know her daughters. Now that both Sarah and Ellie were awake it wasn't long before they were both off the monitoring equipment and going from strength to strength.

'Is it Ellie's turn for a bottle or is she due for me to feed her?' Sheena asked him over Sarah's cries, as she finished changing Ellie's nappy. Will was about to put Sarah into the bath and was ensuring that the clear protective, water-proof bandage was secure over the wound site. Sarah, however, wasn't enjoying being stripped naked and was quite vocal about it.

'Sarah's due for the bottle after her bath. You feed Ellie while I wrangle this minx into the bath.' As he spoke, he bent down and blew a raspberry on Sarah's tummy, surprising the little one so much she was actually quiet for a split second before resuming her cries. He chuckled, the warm sound washing over Sheena with delight as she settled in the chair with Ellie. Unbuttoning her top, she settled the baby to her breast, then looked over to where Will was carefully lifting Sarah into the bath, the baby splashing a bit to begin with before settling down to the soothing warmth of the water.

'Phew!' Will looked down at the little girl. 'You certainly have a good set of lungs, sweet Sarah,' he told her, and was rewarded with a smile. He looked over to where Sheena was feeding Ellie, surprised to find her watching him. Sheena smiled.

'Peace and quiet…if only for a moment. Ah, Sarah, I envy you. What I wouldn't give for a relaxing bath.' Sheena closed her eyes and leaned her head back against the chair. 'Even for ten minutes, just to soak and unwind and have no demands on my time.' She opened her eyes and smiled at Will. 'I guess being a single mother to two little munchkins, my bath dreams are over.

At least for the next five years until they start school.' She chuckled to herself.

Will nodded, listening to her words and mesmerised by the sight of her sitting there, babe in arms, looking so incredibly beautiful and serene. It was clear that she loved her daughters very much and there was no hint of the fears she'd confessed to him almost a week ago outside the operating theatre. He knew they were still there, simmering beneath the surface, but he also knew that she was internally strong enough to cope with whatever life threw at her.

Sarah splashed, demanding his attention once more, and he gave it, murmuring sweet words to her. Both girls had come along in leaps and bounds since the surgery almost a week ago and he couldn't have been happier with their progress.

Ellie was starting to close her eyes, her little world peaceful and content. Sheena was starting to feel the same. Ever since the surgery she'd felt as though she could now start to move forward with her life. It wouldn't be too much longer until the girls would be allowed to go home…

but first she had to find a home for them to go to.

'We'll get there, won't we, my beautiful Eleanor?' she murmured, stroking her baby's head.

'I've never heard you call her Eleanor before,' Will remarked, glancing over. 'How did you choose their names? Any particular reason?'

Sheena nodded, sadness creeping into her eyes. 'Ellie and Sarah were the names of my imaginary sisters when I was growing up.'

'Imaginary?' There was no censure in Will's tone, only intrigue.

'When I was at boarding school, especially during the holidays when all the other girls went home to their families and I was left to rattle around the property all on my own, I used to imagine I had two older sisters who would be there, too. The three of us would go off into the woods around the boarding house and we'd explore together and have wonderful adventures.' Sheena smiled at the memory of her schoolgirl dreams. 'Then at night I'd imagine that they'd push their beds next to mine, one on either side to protect me, so I wasn't all alone in the large empty dormitory.'

'How old were you?'

'About six or seven.'

Will's heart constricted at her words, feeling empathy for little Sheena and anger at her parents for leaving her all alone.

'As I grew older, I would still imagine quiet yet determined Ellie and loud, protective Sarah by my side, always in the back of my mind for whenever I needed them most. I have no idea where I initially pulled the names from but when I knew I was having twin girls, those were the two names that seemed to fit perfectly. My girls—only this time, it would be me who would always protect them.'

Will looked away from her, swallowing the lump that had lodged in his throat. He glanced down at Sarah, still happily splashing away, and discovered his vision was a little blurry. 'Why did you never tell me any of this? About your childhood?' he asked.

Sheena shrugged. 'I guess for so long I didn't want to remember. It was a time in my life I tried hard to forget. Besides, you used to tell me the most wonderful stories about your family, about your siblings and the mischief you used to get up to, and it was all so alive and colourful and real. It helped push the bleakness of my own childhood further into the back of my mind and it's only been recently, since I've had the girls, that I find I can think back to that time without being swamped with feelings of complete desolation and rejection. That time is gone. I can't get it back. I have to look forward. I have a future with my girls and I want it to be bright and alive and colourful. Filled with love and laughter.'

Will nodded in approval. 'That's the way to do it. Move forward.'

There was a strength to his words that made Sheena wonder whether he'd been referring to something other than her childhood memories. She watched as he took Sarah from the bath and wrapped the little girl carefully in the towel, picking her up to cuddle her dry. He was so good with both the girls and it was clear as Sarah snuggled into him that they were both becoming attached to him.

Was that a good thing? She knew Will was only supposed to be working at Adelaide Mercy for another month before he was scheduled to return to Philadelphia. Would he return? Would he stay here and accept the job Charisma had offered him?

On the day after Sarah had woken up, the CEO had headed up the press conference, with the media being allowed to photograph both girls, lying in their separate cribs, and the hospital staff who had been responsible for the life-changing surgery. When Charisma had been giving her report, she'd mentioned to the press that she was hopeful of securing the services of Dr William Beckman for the next two years but they had yet to work out the details of the contract.

Since then Will hadn't mentioned it to Sheena and she hadn't wanted to ask or pry. The friend-ship they were both working hard to maintain was still so new and she didn't want to pressure him one way or the other. Whatever he decided, whether to stay or go, had to be his own decision and she would respect whatever he chose. Would he consider staying in Adelaide as moving forward with his life? She hoped so because having him around, talking to him, sharing these special moments with her girls, was something she'd come to quickly treasure.

'Speaking of moving forward...' he remarked, clearing his throat, and Sheena could sense uncertainty in him. It was in the way he straightened his shoulders, pushing them back and raising his chin slightly, that helped her to recognise the feeling. His firm arms still securely held a squirming Sarah but even though her daughter wriggled, there was no danger of Will dropping her.

'How would you feel about taking the girls out of the hospital tomorrow?' He turned back to the change bench and laid Sarah down, quickly fixing a disposable nappy into place, ensuring the bandaged area was thoroughly dry.

'Out?' Sheena was surprised by this suggestion. 'Oh...um...I hadn't even thought about that.'

'You've been cooped up in this room for well over a week.'

Sheena carefully switched Ellie to the other

breast and when her daughter was once again settled, she glanced up at Will. 'Do you think it's all right to take them out? Where would we go? What would we do? How would we get there? I don't have a car.'

'Whoa, there.' Will chuckled as he finished dressing Sarah, who was once again squirming and registering her displeasure at being dressed. 'Don't go stressing about this, Sheena. For a start, I think the girls are both perfectly well enough to head outside. Tomorrow is supposed to be a nice day, not too hot, not too cold, and I thought perhaps we could start with the park. A walk. In the sunshine. A bit of fresh air and Vitamin D.'

'But I don't have a pram.'

'The hospital has one. Even a twin pram so the girls can be propped up and take a look at what's going on around them.'

Sheena's mind was working overtime, puzzling its way through scenarios.

'If you think it's too soon—' he began, but Sheena held up a hand to stop his words.

'I'm just trying to work things through. I'd

need to pack a bag for each of them. Change of clothes, extra nappies, express some milk. It'll be a lot of work. A lot of preparation.'

'True.' He lifted a bathed and dressed Sarah into his arms and came to sit in the chair next to her. 'Twins are a lot of work and require a lot of preparation. Going out, for even an hour, means you pack the same amount of clothes and paraphernalia as you would if you were going out for the day.'

'How do you know so much about what to pack and how to change nappies and bath squirming little girls?'

'I used to help my mother with my younger siblings. I think I first changed my brother's nappy when I was about six or seven. It was disgusting but that's the way things went in a large family. The older ones helped to care for the younger ones.'

'Sounds great.' Sheena smiled at him, watching as he held Sarah in his arms, the little mischief-maker blowing raspberries and waving her arms about with joy. Ellie could hear her sister and started to wriggle, trying to see what was going on. Sheena eventually gave up and laid Ellie over her knee in order to expel any wind.

Sarah leaned towards her sister, arms held out towards her, as Ellie reached for her twin. Will quickly laid Sarah on his knee so both girls were lying on their stomachs, holding hands across the small gap between the two chairs.

'They love each other,' Sheena remarked. 'No matter what else happens in their lives, they'll always have each other, and that makes me very happy.' She exhaled slowly, then looked at Will. 'OK. Let's take them out tomorrow.'

'I can see you're concerned and I know it's a big step for you,' Will soothed. 'But the girls are healthy enough for this next adventure.'

'So long as we don't get hounded by any press and we can just enjoy ourselves, I think you're right that it's time for an adventure of a different kind. One that doesn't involve a trip to either the operating room or Radiology.'

'Agreed, and they'll be safe in the care of their loving orthopaedic surgeon and their paediatric mother. No dramas.'

'Promise?' Sheena reached out her free hand

to him and he instantly took it, squeezing it with reassurance.

He nodded with determination. 'Promise.'

Later that evening, as Sheena sat in the chair, Sarah feeding in her arms, she thought about Will. He'd been so close, so attentive, so wonderful to her and the girls these past few days. Although she'd had many other friends stopping by to help out, Will's presence had made a difference *to her*.

She knew he was their surgeon, that he was obliged to visit them, to make sure their wounds were healing nicely, but after the kisses they'd shared, Sheena had started to open up to the old feelings she'd tried to hide from. Will had been a major part of her life and for so long she'd tried to repress the way he'd made her feel, but now… was it right to want him back in her life? Would she get hurt again? Would the girls? It was clear they loved him, especially Sarah, who always seemed to calm more quickly whenever she was in Will's arms.

'You've got good taste,' Sheena whispered to

her daughter as the baby finished her evening meal. Ellie was still sleeping but would no doubt wake for her feed the instant Sarah was finished. She knew she'd never be bored, raising twins on her own. There would be always something that needed to be done.

She closed her eyes as she thought about Will's idea of taking the girls to the park the next day, feelings of panic racing through her. She knew she'd become institutionalised, having been confined to the walls of the hospital grounds for such a long time, and that even heading to the park for a few hours would do her and the girls the world of good, but she couldn't help the feeling of apprehension that had ripped through her when Will had first suggested it.

'They'll be safe...' She could hear his voice so clearly in her mind, picture his face before her, breathe in his scent all around her. Sheena sniffed again, then frowned as she realised she really *could* detect his earthy scent. Opening her eyes, a smile came instantly to her lips as she saw him standing there...with one hand behind his back.

'Hi. I didn't hear you come in.'

'I wasn't sure whether you were asleep or not. Sarah is.' Will looked down at the baby sleeping contentedly in her mother's arms without a care in the world.

'I was just thinking,' she murmured, and stood, carrying Sarah back to her crib. 'How about you? How has the rest of your day been? Still writing up my girls' operation for a journal article?'

'The article is coming along nicely.' He waited, trying not to be impatient to give her the surprise he'd spent the better part of the last two hours organising. He was starting to feel like a kid at Christmas!

She tucked the blankets around the sleeping babe, being careful of the bandaging before turning to face him. 'I'm excited and nervous about tomorr—' She stopped. 'Will? Why are you holding a loofah behind your back?'

'Darn. You saw it.' He held out the loofah, which was on the end of a smooth wooden stick. 'It's for you.'

'Uh…thanks…' Sheena accepted the gift, not

at all sure what was going on. 'I'm a little confused. Are you saying that I smell?' She sniffed her clothes. 'You're probably right. With stuff coming out both ends of the girls, it's no wonder I stink.'

'Stuff? Is that the technical term the paediatric association is using nowadays?'

Sheena laughed. 'Yes, as a matter of fact it is, and you were supposed to say, "You don't stink, Sheena." But instead you nitpick my vocabulary, which I might add may not be all that coherent at this time of night.'

'Will you be quiet? I'm trying to give you a present here and you're rambling on.'

'The loofah is my present?' She looked at the item in her hands and gave it the consideration Will obviously thought it deserved. 'Then again, I thank you and promise to use it for my lightning-quick shower tomorrow morning. Honestly, since the girls were born I've learned the true meaning of "quick" showers. Usually, they're both nice and calm until I'm standing naked in the bathroom about to turn on the water and then you can bet they *both* wake up and start crying. It's a conspiracy.' She shook the loofah at him.

'You really are nervous about tomorrow, aren't you?' Will stated, humour laced with impatience in his tone. 'You're babbling faster than a brook. Now, if you'll just listen, I'll explain about the significance of the loofah.'

'Oh. The loofah has significance?'

'It does.'

There was a brief knock at the door and a moment later Raquel-Maria came in. 'You wanted to see me, Will?' she asked.

'Yes. Would you mind keeping an eye on the girls for about three minutes, please?' With that, he took Sheena's free hand in his and gently pulled her from the room. 'Bring the loofah,' he instructed.

'How did Raquel-Maria know to come in then?' Sheena asked as she glanced at her babies before allowing Will to tow her from the room.

'I asked her to give me five minutes just before I came in.'

'Will? Where are we going?' Sheena asked as she walked along beside him, loofah still in her free hand. 'And why did I need to bring the loofah?' They walked down a long corridor towards the maternity ward.

'Because I've organised a surprise for you,' he said as they walked into Maternity. They received some odd looks from people, some smiling, some intrigued, some just confused…much like her. 'The maternity ward is the only place where there are baths,' he said as he held open a door that led to one of the private bathrooms.

Sheena went through and then stopped, her eyes wide with complete surprise. In the room was a decent-size tub filled with sweet-scented bubbles. There were no lights on in the room because it had been lit with about a hundred—or so it seemed—little tea-candles. A nice new fluffy towel hung over the rail and next to it was a large fluffy robe and fluffy slippers. The lights from the candles seemed to twinkle brightly, making the room cosy and relaxed.

'For you,' he murmured. 'You mentioned earlier today that you probably wouldn't be able to enjoy a bath for at least the next five years. I decided that was too long for you to wait. You've been under enormous stress lately and now that both girls are well on the road to recovery, I think you're overdue for some "Sheena" time.'

'But…' Sheena was gobsmacked. She looked from the bath to the glowing candles back to Will. 'I…have to feed Ellie.'

'I've checked the fridge and there's more than enough milk there for Ellie, which means you can definitely spend some time soaking in the tub and letting all your stress and cares go.'

'You're going to…look after my girls?' Sheena was still trying to come to terms with what he'd arranged.

'If you're OK with that, yes. I love spending time with your girls, Sheena. Please let me do this for you.'

Sheena looked at the glorious bubble bath again, almost itching to slip into the soothing water and let all her stresses go. 'I can't believe you've done this for me.' She held up the loofah. 'An incredible bubble bath complete with my own personal loofah.' She giggled, still somewhat surprised at this unexpected turn of events.

'You deserve it, Mother of Adelaide's previously conjoined twins.' Will raised her hand to his lips and pressed a slow, soft kiss to her skin. 'Take all the time you need but, above all, relax.'

He released her hand and stepped from the room, leaving her in peace. Sheena stood there for a moment, breathing in the glorious sweet scents surrounding her and noticing some other little treats Will had prepared in the room. Off to the side of the bath was a small table with a plastic champagne flute and a bottle of non-alcoholic wine. Sheena poured herself a glass and took a soothing sip before stripping off and sliding into the water.

As the bubbles and water surrounded her body, she closed her eyes and sighed, unable to recall a time when she'd been afforded such a luxury as a soak in a tub. The stresses of the past few months started to slip away, her thoughts relaxing along with her body.

Will couldn't have given her a more gracious and precious gift other than some time to herself. He was quite a man and her feelings towards him were intensifying with each passing moment.

* * *

Will was standing by the cribs, watching the girls as they slept, when Sheena walked back into the room almost twenty minutes later. She was dressed in the fluffy robe and slippers, the towel and her clothes folded neatly in her arms.

'Wow.' She stopped just inside the door, gasping at the sight before her. Just as he'd done with the bathroom, Will had placed small tea-light candles around the room. There weren't nearly as many here but it still managed to create a romantic, relaxed atmosphere and Sheena couldn't believe how excited that made her feel. 'It looks… incredible in here, too.'

'I'm glad you like it,' Will murmured, pleased with her response to his idea. He picked up a tea light in his hand and a moment later the light went off.

'How did you do that?'

'They're battery operated. There was no way I was going to risk real candles in here, not with the girls so close.' He switched the candle back on and placed it on the shelf. 'I saw that same thought flick across your face just now, concerned the candles were too close to the girls.'

He took a few slow steps forward, coming to stand in front of her before he leaned in to whisper something near her ear. 'I know your expressions all too well, Dr Woodcombe.' It had been a mistake to lean in close. He'd known it would be because the glorious scent from her bath hung all around her, but he hadn't been able to resist. He eased back, putting a bit more distance between them, and she came further into the room, placing her things on a nearby table before going to check on her girls.

'Both sleeping soundly. Sarah hasn't woken. Ellie finished her bottle about ten minutes ago and she's been changed and settled, as you can see.'

Sheena bent and kissed both her daughters then tucked the fluffy robe closer around her body, conscious not only of the fact that she was naked beneath but also that Will would know that as well.

'Now, why don't you go and get changed while I set up the next part of the surprise?'

'There's more?' Sheena's eyebrows rose in disbelief. 'Will, you don't have to do this. The bath, the candles, the—'

He stepped forward and pressed his finger to her lips. 'Stop trying to control everything. Just for the next hour, while the girls continue to sleep, let yourself continue to relax.'

Sheena edged back a fraction, her lips suffusing with heat where his finger had touched her, and the sensation started to spread throughout the rest of her body. Perhaps Will was right. Perhaps putting on some clothes was the best way for her to feel a little less self-conscious, but she also needed a few moments away from him to pull herself together.

'OK. Good idea.' She quickly crossed to the dresser by Sarah's crib and extracted some clean clothes from her pile. 'Won't be a moment,' she said, heading into the small bathroom attached to the girls' room. It only housed a shower, toilet and handbasin. No big, glorious bath. Once she had changed, still deciding to wear the cute fluffy slippers, she stepped back into the room—and stopped.

Not only were the tea-light candles twinkling

their lights around the room but Will had pushed the chairs to the side, and spread a red-and-black checked picnic rug over the hard floor. A few cushions were scattered around the edge of the rug and in the middle was a cheese and fruit platter, a plate of mini-muffins and some biscuits. Will stood at the door to the room, accepting a tray with a pot of tea and two bone china cups from Raquel-Maria.

He turned and saw her standing there, surveying his handiwork. 'Oh. You're out faster than I'd anticipated. Never mind. Sit down. Make yourself comfortable.' He carried over the tea-tray and knelt down on the rug.

'How…did you do all this? The food? The cushions?' Sheena shook her head in bemusement as she sat down on a cushion and snagged a grape from the platter.

Will smiled but slowly shook his head. 'I'm a man of mystery and never divulge my secrets.'

Sheena laughed and settled more comfortably on the cushions. 'It's been…amazing, Will. The loofah, the bath, some time away from the girls, and now *this*.' She waved a hand at the late-night supper spread before them and sighed. 'Thank you.' Her tone was filled with sincerity. 'For… everything.'

Will heard the honesty in her words as well as the appreciation. 'It was most definitely my pleasure, Sheena Andromeda.'

She giggled at the name. 'I can't believe you remember *that*.'

He seemed surprised. 'The day that you decided to choose your own middle name because you weren't given one? Yes, my dear Dr Woodcombe, I do,' he remarked as he handed her a plate. As she put some food onto it, he spoke quietly.

'We'd just finished a gruelling shift—me in Theatres, you with an epidemic in the children's ward. We sat outside the front of the hospital, looking up at the stars, talking softly about our night. You told me that one child you'd been caring for had three middle names and that you had none.'

Sheena's smile was bright. 'And you told me to choose one. "Choose a name, Sheena. Anything you like and tonight I will christen you with your new name". That's what you said.'

Will lay down on his side, propping himself up on his elbow as they revisited the past. 'You laughed, pointed up at the sky and said, "I choose Andromeda".'

'And you immediately christened me Sheena Andromeda Woodcombe.' Shyly she looked down at the food on her plate before meeting his gaze. 'That's one of my favourite memories. When things in my life aren't going the way I'd planned, that's one of the memories I take out, dust off and think about.'

'It's one of my favourite memories, too,' he confessed. They both fell silent, the years they'd been apart disappearing as their familiarity and the sense of ease in each other's company washed over them.

'Life seemed so simple back then.' She sighed, and hugged one of the cushions to her chest, needing some contact, needing to feel close to him but knowing she couldn't possibly ask him to hold her. That would be far too dangerous.

'We were young.'

She nodded. 'Yet we felt so old. We thought we knew everything.'

'But it turns out not nearly as much as we should have.'

'I'm so glad we've been able to start afresh,' Sheena remarked, her gaze flicking between his eyes and his lips. Did the man have any idea just how irresistible she found him?

'So am I,' he murmured, unable to help but notice the way she was looking at him. Now that they'd sorted through a lot of their past, he was well aware of the mounting tension coursing between them. He'd kissed her twice—almost three times—and having that small sweet taste of Sheena had only unlocked the cravings he'd kept hidden away for far too long.

'Don't look at me like that, Sheena,' he whispered quietly into the sudden stillness of the room, the only sound that of two little girls breathing deeply as they slept.

'Then you shouldn't have given me such a wondrous evening, Will. No one has ever done something so unselfish for me. Usually, whenever I get a treat, there are strings attached.' She frowned for a second and looked at him with concern in her eyes. 'There aren't any strings attached, are there?'

He thought about her parents, about the boarding school, about her ex-husband, and how it honestly did seem as though Sheena had lived her life always waiting for the axe to fall. Well, not with him. 'Only that I like seeing you smiling, seeing you relaxed and being able to unwind after everything you've been through.'

'And that's it?'

'That's it.' He sat up and faced her, knowing it was best to ease the tension surrounding them. 'Now, before the girls start to wake up, can I interest you in some cheese? Or perhaps milady would like some more grapes. A mini-muffin, perhaps?'

'You've organised way too much food,' she said with a laugh, pleased he'd managed to break the intense atmosphere. She wanted him. There were no two ways about it but she also knew it was completely the wrong time of her life to be worrying about romance. Friendship—now, that was something she could handle, and for the next fifteen minutes they sipped tea and nibbled at the food until Sarah woke up, demanding their attention.

All in all, though, when Will finally took his leave after helping her to pack away the rug and set up her camp bed for the night, Sheena couldn't resist standing on tiptoe and kissing his cheek.

'You're a *good* man, Will Beckman, with an equally *good* heart. That's a rare quality nowadays. Thank you again for my wonderful and relaxing evening.'

Will shoved his hands into his pockets to stop himself from hauling her close but smiled and nodded. 'You're more than welcome. Now, get some sleep because tomorrow is another big day, both for you and the girls.'

'And I'm so happy that you'll be there to share it with us.'

'There you are.' Miles walked over to where Will was sitting in the hospital cafeteria, the smells of bacon, eggs, sausages and grilled tomatoes filling the air. Miles pulled out a chair and sat down next to his friend, giving him closer scrutiny. Unshaven, crumpled shirt, no tie. 'I've been looking for you. Aren't you supposed to be taking Sheena and the girls out for a few hours?'

Will frowned and glanced at his watch. 'I'm not due to meet her for another hour.' He looked more closely at his watch and then checked one of the clocks on the wall in the cafeteria. 'What? My watch battery must have died.' He quickly finished his half-drunk coffee and rose to his feet. 'Did she ask you to come and find me? Is everything all right? Are the girls fine? I checked on them just after two o'clock this morning and they both seemed fine.'

Miles raised an eyebrow, taking in his friend's attire. 'Interesting look you have there. Is it the new dishevelled surgeon look you were after? Because I think you've achieved it.'

'I couldn't sleep. Too much on my mind.'

'You've been out walking, haven't you?' Miles asked rhetorically, knowing his friend of old. The two men headed out of the cafeteria, talking as they walked. 'Your all-night walking and thinking escapades usually only happen when you can't figure things out. Now, I know the twins are fine because I've already been around to see them, so that can only mean it's their mother who's been keeping you awake. She's clearly messing with your mind.'

'How do you even know what's in my mind?' Will spluttered, and became even more annoyed when Miles had the audacity to chuckle.

'Because I've been in your position, mate. If it's love that's bothering you, don't even try to work it out.' They rounded the corner into a longer corridor and continued their way to the paediatric unit. 'I tried to fight love and look...' He held up his left hand, where a gold wedding band gleamed. He laughed again. 'I've never been more happy in my life. Janessa is... everything I've ever wanted in a woman and, where for years I thought I'd never find happiness again, it jumped up and slapped me right between the eyes the instant I saw her.'

'You think I've fallen in love with Sheena?'

Miles snorted. 'I don't think you ever *stopped* loving her. She may have broken your heart ten years ago but back then she thought she was doing the right thing, but right or wrong and no matter what you may have been able to trick yourself into believing, it's as plain as the nose on your face that you still love that woman… and her adorable girls.'

'Who *doesn't* love those girls?' Will tried to smooth his crumpled shirt. He'd meant to head back to his parents' house and change his clothes before taking Sheena and the girls out but now he'd run out of time.

'True, but not the way you do. I've seen you with them and both Ellie and Sarah have you wrapped firmly around their tiny fingers. As for their mother—well, whenever you two are in the same room the tension buzzing between you is almost enough to power the entire hospital.'

Will frowned in puzzlement. 'It can't be that obvious.'

'It is to me but, then, I've known both of you for quite some time. I remember what the two of you were like the last time you were together and I can see the same things happening. Those long looks, those meaningful touches, those secret smiles.' Miles over-dramatised his words with wide hand gestures. Will felt a smile start to tug at his lips. 'Add to all of that the fact that I'm a man wildly in love with his wife,' Miles continued, 'and I want every other man to be as happy and as fortunate as I am.'

'And you think I'd be happy with Sheena?'

'I think the only time you've ever truly been happy was when you were with Sheena. Which brings me to my next question.'

Will stopped and faced his friend. 'Don't ask it. I've been asking myself all night long how I really feel about her and I still haven't come up with any answers, only more questions.' The main question was whether he'd be content not to have any natural children of his own. He loved both Sarah and Ellie as though they were his own. With the amount of time he'd spent with them, it was now second nature for him to change them or give them a bottle or simply cuddle them.

Sheena hadn't restricted him in any way, accepting his help and advice, but he could still see concern in her eyes. She wasn't sure whether he was going to stay in Australia or whether he was going to go back to the States. He hadn't been able to talk to her about it because he wasn't sure himself…yet.

'All right, then,' Miles continued. 'Let me ask you this question. How do you feel when you think of her spending her life with someone else?' Miles received an immediate growl as his answer.

'I can't even go there,' Will confessed, his jaw clenched, his fists tight, his heart instantly in pain.

'Interesting.' They started walking again, drawing closer to the paediatric unit. 'You and Sheena are good together, Will, but communication wasn't your strong suit ten years ago—on both sides. Don't let it hold you back this time.'

'I don't intend to. I want to be part of their lives,' Will said as they stopped just outside the door to the paediatric unit.

'But?' Miles prompted.

'What if Sheena can't have any more children? What if Ellie and Sarah are it?'

Miles nodded. 'And there goes your big family picture.'

'I know it might sound pathetic but I always pictured myself surrounded by a lot of children.'

'What about adoption? If Sheena can't have any more children, how about considering it? There are many children out there just waiting to be loved.'

Will nodded but didn't make any remark. Instead, he opened the door to the unit and instantly heard a baby crying.

'That's Sarah,' he said, quickening his pace.

'How can you tell? Just from a cry?' Miles was totally amazed.

'Sarah's cry is deeper than Ellie's and a heck of a lot louder, too.' Will entered the room and found Sheena trying to quickly finish dressing Ellie, calling to Sarah in a soothing tone.

'I'm coming, Sarah,' she said. 'Mummy's almost finished. Shh, darling.'

'Hey. Sorry I'm late.' Will headed to Sarah's crib, his heart turning over when she instantly held out her arms to him, wanting him to pick her up. No sooner was she in his arms than her cries subsided and she snuggled into him. Will closed his eyes and hugged the little girl tight. She was *his* Sarah, just as Ellie was *his* Ellie.

And Sheena? Was she *his* Sheena? Was he fortunate enough to still have her love him? He hoped so.

CHAPTER EIGHT

As THEY headed out into the sunshine, Will pushing the pram with ease, Sheena slipped her sunglasses on and made sure the little sunhats were shielding the girls' eyes properly. Will slipped the hood of the pram into place and breathed in the fresh air.

'They're both blinking rapidly,' Sheena said with a smile on her face. 'They're not used to being in direct sunlight.'

'All that's going to change. Now that the main surgery is over, they're both going to start moving more and crawling, and before you know it they'll be running around creating more mischief than you can imagine.'

'Oh, help. Don't say that.' Sheena laughed. 'I feel so silly for being nervous about bringing them outside.'

'You're nervous?' he asked as they headed towards the botanical gardens situated near the hospital.

'I know. I guess it's because all they've known of life are the four walls of the hospital.'

'They've never been outside before?'

Sheena shook her head. 'Although they were healthy before the surgery, the risk of being outside, of catching a cold or getting sick in some way, was just too great. Miles and Janessa were in complete agreement and none of us wanted to make any mistakes in case it delayed the surgery. Besides, when they were conjoined, they were such a media novelty that even when *I* went out of the hospital grounds I was often photographed and asked questions.'

'So this is their very first time?' He nodded, feeling proud that he was here for such a momentous occasion.

'Yes.'

'Then you have every right to be silly or nervous or whatever other maternal emotions you feel.' He winked at her as he pushed the pram along and Sheena felt sparkly inside from his attention. It had always been that way with Will.

He just needed to look at her, smile at her and her body came alive with tingles.

She quickly looked away and focused on the girls, making sure they were comfortable. Due to the bandages, the girls were unable to sit up properly but they'd angled both babies so that they could see quite clearly the world around them.

Sheena held open the gate to the gardens as Will pushed the pram through and as they walked around she couldn't help but feel as though a huge weight had been lifted from her shoulders.

'I've been so scared,' she confessed to Will as they found a nice place to spread a rug and sit down, the girls content to remain in the pram. They faced the pram towards them and as Sheena talked, Will pulled faces at the girls, making them giggle. 'Trying to imagine my life outside the hospital gave me nightmares.'

'That's understandable.'

'It is?'

'Of course.' Will handed the girls a soft toy each and turned to face Sheena. 'Your life has been in a state of flux for the past year. Now that the girls have come through the surgery, your life with them can begin. Coming out today was the first step towards looking to the future, and you've accomplished it with ease.' He leaned over and took her hand in his, raising it to his lips. 'You're a strong, incredible woman, Sheena Woodcombe, and you'll be able to handle anything life throws at you.'

Sheena nodded, tingling from his touch, loving the attention but well aware that in the way he spoke he wasn't including himself in any scenario. Did that mean he wasn't going to stay in Australia? Was he going to return to the States but didn't know how to break it to her? They'd agreed to be friends and even though there was a high level of tension buzzing between them whenever they were in the same room, both had been conscious of not following through on it. Re-establishing their friendship had been the most important thing but Sheena had been well aware that with every moment she'd spent with him, whether it was bathing and changing or feeding the girls, she was coming to rely on him more and more. So much so that when he left, when he exited her life, she'd be left with a gaping hole of sheer emptiness that she doubted she'd ever be able to fill.

Even thinking about it now made a lump form in her throat and she looked away from him, over into the trees around them. She sat up straighter, her attention captured by a person hiding behind one of the trees. Her eyes widened when she realised he had a camera and that a large telephoto lens was pointed in their direction.

'The media.'

'What about them?' Will asked, noting the change in her demeanour.

'They're over there.' Sheena shook her head, annoyed that the very first time she'd brought the girls out of the hospital, they'd been followed. Her first instinct was to pack everything up and return to the sanctuary of the hospital as fast as possible but she'd learned through her PR briefings that it was better to face the music and give the photojournalists the scoop they were after.

'Relax,' Will said softly. 'We'll invite him over.

He can take his pictures and then we'll be left alone.'

Sheena nodded. 'Agreed, but I don't like it. My daughters aren't a sideshow.'

'No. They're two little girls who have captured the hearts of many,' Will said. 'Including me.' He pulled Sheena to her feet and embraced her in a protective hug, not caring who saw them. 'I'll be right by your side,' he reassured her. 'No one's going to hurt my girls.'

Within another minute Sheena found herself standing behind the pram with Will by her side as they smiled for the camera, the photojournalist as pleased as punch to be allowed to take his photographs. The whole time she smiled, Will's last words were running around in her head. *'No one's going to hurt* my *girls.'* Did that mean that he'd accepted them? That he wanted them? All three of them? Hope began to increase deep within her.

'Make sure you send us a copy,' Will said as he started to wheel the pram back towards the hospital. By the time they arrived back in the paediatric unit, Sheena was mentally exhausted and so were the girls. With Will's help, she settled them in their cribs, singing a lullaby to help them drift off to sleep.

'I think that's enough excitement for one day,' she murmured, delighted when Will brought her a soothing cup of herbal tea. 'You remembered.'

'Of course I remembered. Whenever we were working nights, you used to complain that you never got to have your soothing cup of herbal tea.'

'I never complained,' she said, going to the window to look out at the sunny afternoon. Will came to stand beside her, sipping his own cup of tea.

'I beg to differ.' He chuckled, the warm sound washing over her. She turned slightly, putting her cup on the thick window ledge between the vases of flowers still blooming brightly.

'Will?'

'Yes?'

'What's happening between us?'

He smiled at her words. 'We're being friends.'

'I know, and I like it very much, but…' She didn't have to say another word as he put his cup down and pulled her into his arms. Closing her eyes, she rested her head against his chest, listening to the steady beat of his heart.

'We're at a crossroads, Sheena.' She felt him shake his head. 'Not just as a possible couple but as singles as well. I have big decisions to make. You have big decisions to make, and in some ways, until those decisions are made, we won't know how to move forward.'

Sheena opened her eyes and looked up at him. 'How about you make my decisions and I'll make yours? That way, the pressure can be off,' she suggested with a crazy smile.

He looked at her and returned her smile. 'If only it was that simple.'

'Seriously, though, is there anything I can help with? Any questions you want answered? We weren't too good at communicating properly all those years ago, so let's make sure we don't take that road again.'

Will thought about things for a while before nodding. 'OK. Well, I do have a few questions. The first one being about your endometriosis.

Are you in any pain? Will you need further surgery?'

Sheena eased out of his arms and saw the concern on his face. 'The pain isn't too bad, nowhere near as bad as it used to be, and, yes, there's a high probability that I'll require an oophorectomy, possibly a bilateral one, which will mean definitely no more children for little ol' me.'

'Oh, Sheenie.' There was anguish in his eyes. 'How do you put up with it? Always to be in pain and knowing that with surgical intervention the pain can be removed? You're so brave, so strong.' And he wanted to hold her for ever and take away all her pain. He wanted to protect her and her girls for the rest of his life.

'I put up with it because now that I've had the girls, I'm incredibly hopeful. I want more children, Will. I feel incredibly greedy saying that, especially as I've already been blessed with two gorgeous girls, but…' She trailed off. She wanted more children, almost desperately so, and she wanted them to be Will's. Hers and his. Just as she'd dreamed about all those years ago.

'The doctors were wrong about me before and perhaps…just perhaps they're still wrong when they say there's an incredibly small chance of me conceiving again. So I put up with the pain and I'll continue to do so if it means that there's a tiny chance.'

'So long as your health isn't at risk.' They both knew the risks. 'The chance of conceiving is irrelevant if it means you become sick.' He shook his head. 'The thought of you—' He broke off, unable to say the words out loud. Instead, he put his hands on her shoulders and looked deeply into her eyes. 'You're too important, Sheena. To your girls, to Janessa and Miles…and to me.' He swallowed the lump in his throat. 'Promise me you'll look after yourself.'

Sheena met his gaze, unable to believe the intenseness of his blue eyes. 'I promise.'

'Good.' He breathed out in relief before crushing her to him. 'You are so special to me, Sheena. So incredibly special.'

'As a friend?' she asked, and he eased her back to look down into her upturned face.

'Not *just* as a friend, and I think we both know

that.' A small smile tugged at his mouth. 'I've found it difficult to keep my hands off you ever since I returned to Australia, but I knew I had to.'

'We needed to talk.'

'And we did. I want us to stay on the same page, Sheena, to be constantly communicating with each other.'

'I want that, too, Will. I'm still so sorry for what happened all those years ago and for the way I handled things, but—'

Will didn't want to hear her apologies so silenced her the best way he knew how and covered her mouth with his own. Sheena gasped in surprise then leaned into him, relaxing against his body, winding her arms about his neck. Closing her eyes, she knew this was the place she'd longed to be for such an incredibly long time. In Will's arms once more. Being kissed with more than a brief brush of his lips against hers. This was real. *This* was what she'd dreamed about.

Her mouth was smooth and warm and, oh, so ready for him. It was as though her lips had been made specifically for *him* to kiss, and he was relishing every second. Their scents mingled together as he slowly slid his hands up her back, drawing her as close as he possibly could. When she groaned, he took that as an invitation to increase the intensity of the kiss.

Her mouth opened beneath his and they went on a mutual journey of becoming reacquainted. It was exciting, enthralling and exhilarating, and she couldn't get enough. Never before had his kisses made her feel like this, and she realised that there was definitely something different. Was it maturity? They'd both been through a lot in the past ten years and that had to change a person. He felt so familiar and yet so different, and it was that difference that made her eager to explore, to know more of this new Will who had once again captured her heart.

His kisses continued to turn her entire body to mush and she leaned closer into him, not only wanting his firm body pressed against her own but to find more stability to keep her from sliding to the floor in a boneless mess.

It was Will's turn to groan as he continued to hold her close, still giving and receiving in equal portions, feeding his need. She was everything he remembered and more, and finally, when he thought his lungs would burst if he didn't drag oxygen into them, he reluctantly lifted his head from hers but didn't relinquish his hold on her delectable body.

With their breathing slowly returning to normal, Sheena looked up at him. 'Wow!'

'Yeah. Wow. I mean, it was always good between us but that was…'

'Different.'

'But good different,' he confirmed, and she nodded in agreement.

'Wh-what are we supposed to do now? Where does that incredibly sexy, incredibly passionate kiss leave us?'

'Shaken,' he replied with a laugh, but let her go to pace the room, pleased the girls were still sleeping soundly. 'I have to decide whether to accept Charisma's job offer or to continue with my work and research in the States. You have to decide where you want to live, where you want to put down roots with your girls. We need to decide whether to pursue this undeniable attraction or to pull back and just remain friends.'

Sheena covered her face with her hands. 'Why can't anything in my life be simple?' she asked rhetorically, before lowering her hands and stepping forward into his pacing path.

'What do you think about…dating?'

'Dating?'

'Sure. For the rest of the time you're here in Australia, we still work on our friendship but we date as well. There's no point in denying the attraction between us any more, Will, and it might possibly lead to more confusion, which is the last thing we both want.'

'So we date.' He nodded as though the idea had merit. Where the girls were concerned, they both knew they worked well together, but if they had plans to solidify their relationship, to lead towards marriage, they needed to make sure they were definitely on the same page.

Was it possible he would be able to have the fairy-tale family after all? Himself, Sheena and the girls? Could they make this work? It wasn't the fairy-tale family he'd envisaged all those years ago but did it really matter? Dating might help them both to be sure. He'd rushed into things ten years ago and it had ended in disaster. He wasn't going to be that foolish this time around.

'You're a good catch, Will Beckman.'

He smiled at her words, almost relieved to hear her say them. 'Is that so?'

'Yeah.' She returned his smile, her earlier annoyance and frustration with the media being replaced by a calm, serene sigh that only Will's relaxing presence could evoke. He reached out and cupped her cheek with his hand, his thumb tenderly caressing her soft skin. She leaned into his touch and relaxed.

'So…if we're serious about this dating thing, how do you feel about meeting my family?'

At his words, Sheena jerked her head upright and stared at him.

'Uh…that's a little…uh…quick, isn't it?'

'Sheena?' He spread his arms wide. 'I have to return to the States before Christmas. That's not that far away.'

'True. True.' She took a few calming breaths,

then nodded. 'I guess it's only fair that I meet your family. Especially as you've already met mine. The girls, Janessa and Miles,' she said by way of explanation.

'I guess I have.' He reached for her again, taking her hands in his. 'It'll be fine. My parents will adore you.'

'Are you sure?' Now that he'd suggested the meeting, she couldn't help the nervous butterflies that were zinging around her stomach. 'I've never met anyone's parents before. Jonas's had both died and I hardly knew mine. What am I supposed to do?'

Will smiled at her, surprised at her nervousness yet unable to believe how adorable she looked. 'You be yourself.'

'Do I need to get them a gift? Isn't it customary to bring a gift when you meet parents for the first time?'

Will shrugged. 'Bring the girls. My parents love children and will definitely consider spending some time with Adelaide's star twins a very special gift.'

Sheena nodded and tried once more to calm her breathing. 'Are you sure about this?'

'Positive. If we want to move forward, Sheena, we need to do this.' He leaned forward and brushed one of those rich and tantalising kisses over her mouth. 'Trust me.'

She breathed out slowly, her entire body trembling as she nodded. 'OK.'

CHAPTER NINE

'I'M TERRIFIED!'

Sheena paced around the girls' room before stopping to check that the baby bag was packed with everything she might need. She'd expressed milk, and the bottles were stored in the special milk compartment. There were enough nappies for her to stay away for a week—at least, that was what Janessa had said.

'Relax. You'll be fine,' Janessa soothed.

'I don't know how to meet parents, Ness. I've never met anyone's parents before...well, except for your dad.'

'You know Miles's parents. You met them at the wedding.'

'That's hardly the same. I wasn't in love with their son.'

'I should hope not,' Janessa retorted, then stopped. 'Wait a second. You said...'

'I know what I said and I can't dwell on it right now. Weren't you nervous when you met Miles's parents? What did you do? What did you say? Maybe I can learn something to say.'

Janessa waved her friend's words away. 'You're taking the babies, Sheena. No offence, honey, but no one's going to be interested in you. Babies have that effect on people, especially your two little darlings.'

'Will's hiring a car and the hospital is providing child car seats. This is the first time the girls have travelled in a car. What if we have an accident?'

Janessa walked to her friend and put her hands on her shoulders. 'Will you calm down? Will's parents don't live too far away. It's about a ten-minute drive from the hospital. Everything is going to be fine.'

'Is she still in a flap?' Will asked as he walked into the room.

'Yes. Come and silence her in a way only you know how. I'll take the baby bag down to the car. You two can bring the girls.' Janessa turned and left them alone, Ellie and Sarah were all dressed up in a pair of matching floral dresses, their dark hair tied up with red bows in little fountains on top of their heads. They looked adorable, as did their mother, apart from the flap she was in.

'I have something for you,' Will said, and it was only then Sheena realised he had one hand behind his back.

'Another loofah? This is hardly the time for a bath.'

He laughed. 'That stopped you from stressing for a moment. Here.' He shifted and pulled, from behind his back, a beautiful bouquet of brightly coloured flowers.

'Freesias.' Sheena gasped. 'The biggest bunch I've ever seen. Oh, Will.' She accepted the flowers and bent her head to sniff them appreciatively. 'They're gorgeous. Thank you. Thank you so much.'

Will beamed. 'I know you already have a room full of flowers but these aren't for the girls—these are for you.'

'And I love freesias. They're my favourite.'

'I remember.'

They stood there. Oblivious to anything or

anyone else. Absorbed in each other for what felt like minutes but in reality was only a few seconds. His intense blue gaze was like a visual caress as he took in her comfortable shoes, three-quarter-length designer jeans and a blue shirt that clung to her feminine curves. She looked incredible, her short dark hair framing her face, her blue eyes, her pink cheeks, her plump, kissable lips.

Will swallowed. 'You look stunning, Sheenie.'

She put the flowers down for a moment and then looked at her clothes. 'Are you sure? Because I can go and change if you don't think this is appro—'

Will stepped forward and kissed her. 'I *do* like this method of relaxing you,' he murmured after a moment. 'Let me put these flowers into some water for you and then we'll take the girls down to the car,' he said, reluctantly releasing her from his arms.

A minute later, he walked over to the cribs, where the girls were wide awake.

'Hello, sweet Sarah,' he crooned, and was instantly rewarded with the biggest grin Sheena had ever seen her daughter give anyone. Her daughter had good taste. Sarah waved her arms at Will, desperate to be picked up, and he didn't disappoint her, scooping her up and pressing kisses to her cheeks.

Ellie started to grizzle, which she only did when she thought she was being left out. Sheena instantly collected her daughter and took her over to Will so he could say hello to her. Ellie rewarded him with big smiles and leaned forward, her arms outstretched. Will shifted Sarah over and accepted Ellie as Sheena handed her over.

'They both adore you,' she murmured with a smile.

'The feeling's mutual. Right, time to go.' Will looked at her. 'Ready?'

'As I'll ever be.' She spread her arms wide and let them fall back down to her sides in a gesture of surrender.

'Excellent. Then let us away!'

Janessa was at the car, waiting for them at the front of the hospital. Sheena and Will clipped the girls into their car seats before heading off, waving goodbye to Janessa as Will drove them from the hospital. He reached over and took her hand in his.

'Still OK?'

'Yes. It felt strange the other day when you took us to the gardens but this is…well, this is really giving the girls a taste of normal life.'

Will nodded. 'It happens often to people who have prolonged stays in hospital.' They continued to chat as he drove carefully towards his parents' home. He turned off the main road, heading into an older suburb, the trees high, the gardens lush and green from the recent rain. They passed a little creek with a small play park next to it. Will pointed to it.

'Before they made that area into a park, it was sort of like a mini-quarry and my brothers and I would spend a lot of time playing there, creating imaginary games of intergalactic war, often refusing to allow our sisters into the game at all. Then the girls would run and tell Mum or Dad and we'd be instructed, in the most direct way possible, to allow them to play, and of course the girls used to really mess the game up. Where we boys were content to roll around in the dirt and hide behind the rocks and shrubs for protection against the high-powered laser blasters contained in our index fingers as we tried to save the omniverse from imploding, my sisters wanted to tidy the place up and make delicious mud pies.' He grinned widely. 'It was all very stereotypical.'

Sheena laughed. 'It sounds like…fun.'

'It must have been so difficult for you, growing up alone.' He rubbed his thumb over the back of her hand. The love and trust that ran between himself, his parents and his siblings was incredibly strong and while, over the years, he might not have been able to see them as much as he would have liked, the bond was still there and as strong as ever. He knew his mother would instantly warm to Sheena but would Sheena allow herself to accept such open love? From the little she'd told him about her parents and the lack of affection they'd shown their only daughter, he hoped she really was able to leave it behind her and move forward.

'I can't imagine what it must have been like

for you but of one thing I am absolutely sure, and that's that your daughters will have a fantastic time growing up with you as their mother. They'll laugh and argue and learn how to deal with the world, and you'll be able to enjoy it all with them.'

Sheena felt a tightening in her chest at his words. 'I hope so. It's what I've always wanted from the moment I first discovered I was pregnant.'

'My mother always said that being a parent gives you the chance to enjoy a second childhood,' Will continued, 'and you get to do it with all the knowledge of an adult so you don't make silly mistakes like thinking you can ride your bike off a ramp constructed with some bricks and a plank of wood, and do a loop in the air and land perfectly on two wheels.'

Sheena pushed aside her internal panic and smiled at him. 'You didn't?'

'Oh, I did, and had a cast on my arm for eight weeks to prove it.'

'I'm starting to be thankful I had girls, not boys.'

'Oh, don't let gender fool you. Sarah has enough fight in her to give you a run for your money and Ellie…' He glanced at the girls, who he could see in the rear-view mirror. 'Well, the quiet ones are usually the most stubborn.'

She nodded in agreement. 'You know them so well, Will. I have no idea how I'm going to cope with one girl who's stubborn and one who's a fighter.' He brought the car to a halt outside a charming yet nostalgic brick-veneer home as Sheena once more battled her own insecurities. It didn't appear that she would be able to suppress them, especially when today she would be surrounded by all the reminders of everything she'd missed growing up—a loving family. What Will had said was true. She *did* have the opportunity to have a second childhood, to leave her own upbringing behind and start afresh. Still doubt niggled. 'How am I ever going to cope alone?'

Will switched off the engine and turned to face her. 'You won't be alone, Sheenie.'

It wasn't until he urged her closer that she realised she'd spoken her concern out loud. Will leaned towards her, capturing her lips with his. Sheena's eyelids fluttered closed as she sighed into the kiss, drawing hope and strength and a yearning desire to always have this man in her life, to have him beside her as the father of her children as they lived together for the rest of their lives. Was it possible to believe in such a fairy-tale? Throughout her entire life she'd wanted the fairy-tale, the happily-ever-after ending.

Now here she was, outside the home of Will's parents, with Will close to her, kissing her, making her feel cherished, wanted, needed, loved. She kissed him back with all the love in her heart, wanting him to know that she'd never stopped loving him, that hurting him all those years ago had been the worst moment in her life and that she really wanted nothing else than for the two of them to make a 'proper' family with her girls. It was the fairy-tale…but she knew of old that fairy-tales never came true.

'Sheena,' he whispered against her mouth, their breathing slightly erratic. 'I can't stop thinking about you, wanting you, needing you and—'

'There you two are.' The joyful female tones

cut through the air and Will broke off from what he'd been saying and slowly pulled back, obviously not caring whether his mother had seen them kissing or not. He let go of her hand before climbing quickly from the car to come around to her side and open the door for her.

As Sheena stepped out, his mother came to their side and openly embraced her son. Will hugged his mother back, not at all embarrassed by the display of emotion. Sheena felt a lump rise in her throat at the sight. Will was a grown man but the love and respect he had for his mother was clearly evident. She opened the back door, only to discover that both the girls had enjoyed their first car ride so much that they'd drifted off to sleep.

'They're asleep,' she announced with a hint of incredulity in her tone. 'I mean, I'd heard of parents driving their children around in the car in order to get them to go to sleep but I didn't think that it actually *worked*.'

Will's mother chuckled and stepped forward, peering around Sheena to see into the back seat of the car. 'It's very true, my dear. I remember driving around these very streets with a car full of children, desperate for them to go to sleep so I could at least have some peace and quiet, especially if Stephen was working late. Oh, aren't they adorable? So precious,' she remarked of the twins before turning to face Sheena. She opened her arms wide and wrapped them around Sheena in much the same way that she'd hugged her son. 'And I'm very happy to meet you, too, Sheena.'

In the next instant Sheena found herself enveloped in the warmest, sweetest maternal hug she'd ever experienced. She closed her eyes, wanting to savour every second, the fairy-tale dreams she'd had back in school coming back to life in that one moment. This woman didn't know her at all, yet Sheena felt complete acceptance. Was this how her baby girls felt when she cuddled them? All warm and secure and loved? How wonderful!

'I'm Mary,' Will's mother said as she released Sheena. 'And you are very, very welcome. Now, let me help you get these adorable creatures out so you can come inside. I've already put the kettle on.'

Unsure whether the girls would wake up or stay asleep but knowing she couldn't leave them in the car, Sheena and Will unpacked the pram from the back of the car and then carefully transferred the girls from the car seats to the pram. Thankfully, Sarah stayed asleep but the instant they moved her, Ellie woke up, smiling brightly up at Will.

'Oh, look at the gorgeous smiles on this one,' Mary cooed, and was more than happy to carry the baby bag into the house while Will and Sheena manoeuvred the pram through the door.

'Are you all right?' Will whispered near Sheena's ear once they were inside.

'I'm fine. Why?'

He smiled down into her face. 'You looked a little dazed when my mother hugged you. I probably should have warned you that she's a very demonstrative person.'

Sheena quickly shook her head. 'Oh, I'm not worried about that. I think it's marvellous.' With happiness sparkling in her eyes, she shrugged one shoulder, feeling a little self-conscious. 'It's just that…well…I've never been hugged by anyone's mother before. Not even my own. It was amazing.'

Will stared at her as he comprehended her words. 'You really have no concept of what a family is like, do you?'

'I used to watch Janessa and her father interact, amazed at the way they talked so openly and freely with each other. She took his death pretty hard but with her help I've learned that pulling a family together from people around you can also give you what you need, even if the people aren't blood relatives.'

'And that's your grounding in family life?' He wasn't being critical, he was simply astounded.

'I guess so.'

'Then allow me to show you a different sort of family life. The sort of family life you deserve to have with your girls.'

As they stepped into the front entryway of the house, a loud squeal came from the hallway. A second later a toddler ran past them, quickly followed by a boy of about three. A woman laughed somewhere in the house and a deep masculine voice asked when it was going to be time for a coffee break. Sarah slept on while Ellie looked eagerly around at this new scenery.

The walls of the house were decorated with many different photographs, some in black and white, some in colour and all of them framed with mix-and-match frames. There were vases of flowers on most of the tables and an upright piano in the corner. There were paintings, knick-knacks and lace doilies around the place. So incredibly different from the spacious, impersonal mansion where her parents lived. There had been no personal photographs on the walls there, only expensive artwork. Her mother had only worn the latest in couture whilst Mary wore a comfortable cotton dress with little rosebuds all over it, which definitely matched her sunny disposition.

Will wheeled the pram through to the kitchen, which Sheena soon discovered was the main hub of the house as it contained an enormous wooden family table and ten chairs. A woman was sitting on a stool at the kitchen bench; Mary was calling to her husband, who was busy hammering in the backyard, and children were running everywhere. The smell of a freshly brewed pot of coffee filled the air, along with chocolate-chip cookies, which were cooling on a rack.

As Will rushed forward to greet the woman who she quickly realised was not only one of his sisters but also six months pregnant, Sheena clutched her hands to her chest and nodded. This was right. This was what it should be like. All noise and laughter and smiles and talking, everyone mingling with each other but still somehow understanding what was going on. This was family...a *real* family.

Ellie wriggled, eager to be free from the pram, and Sheena instantly unclipped her from the safety harness. Mary was the first to hold out her hands, eager for a cuddle with the baby. Will instructed his mother on the best way to hold her and how to be careful of the bandaging that was still in place beneath Ellie's pretty cotton dress.

Ten minutes later Sarah awoke on her usual default setting of crying loudly for attention. Thankfully for her, she had plenty of people there just waiting to give it. Stephen begged for a cuddle and, just as she did with Will, Sarah settled almost instantly.

'She likes the men,' Sheena whispered to Will, then frowned humorously. 'That might be a worry one day.'

He chuckled and slipped his arm about her shoulders. 'We'll cope.'

We'll cope? She tried to remain cool, calm and collected at his words, aware that he might not have even realised he'd said 'we'. However, it did make her wonder that even if Will was really serious about their burgeoning relationship, was *she* really ready to move forward?

She wanted Will in her life, almost to the point of desperation, but was she really any good for him? She'd loved him so much all those years ago that she'd had to let him go. She'd known he'd wanted a family and that she hadn't been able to give it to him.

Well, now she *could* give him a family but what if he wanted more children? His sister was pregnant with her fourth child and from the photographs around the house it was clear that his other siblings also had gone forth and multiplied.

There was absolutely no guarantee that she'd ever be able to conceive again. Her doctors had told her that her pregnancy with Ellie and Sarah had been a miracle. Even *they* weren't quite sure how it had happened. It gave her hope. Hope that one day she'd be able to have Will's baby.

Will deserved to have a whole gaggle of children. He deserved to live in a house like this, one filled with photographs and toys and miscellaneous paraphernalia. He deserved this life… and she simply didn't know if she was capable of giving it to him.

CHAPTER TEN

LUNCH with his parents and his sister Anna was such a laid-back, relaxed affair that instead of feeling highly self-conscious, Sheena found herself laughing along with the others. Compared to the stiff dinner parties she'd occasionally been allowed to attend with her parents, the Beckman clan carried on as though they were from another planet. Or perhaps it was *her* upbringing that had been out of this world? What she was experiencing with them was normal and it was the type of upbringing she was determined to give her girls.

Throughout the morning she'd talked with Will's sister, asking about Jesse, who was running about the place, and little Lester, who had only been walking for the past three months. She'd watched Mary give Ellie a bottle and had been astounded when Stephen had offered to change Sarah's nappy.

'Along with Mary, I've raised five of my own and I wasn't one of those old-fashioned fathers who stepped back and let the wife do everything. No, siree. I was in there, changing nappies, bathing babies, cleaning up messes and fixing toys.'

'A hands-on dad,' Sheena had said with a laugh as she'd accepted Sarah so she could feed her. Ellie had been almost done with the bottle and Mary had cradled her carefully, humming a sweet song. Ellie's eyes had closed, content that everything was perfectly fine in her little world.

'Have you had enough milk for both of them?' Anna asked now as she collected Lester and held him on her side, careful to avoid her baby bump.

'I have. I've been very fortunate in that area.'

'That's good. With this one...' she inclined her head towards Lester '...my milk dried up within a month. Then again, he was a whopping ten pounds, seven ounces when he was born *and* he was a week early!'

'A healthy baby indeed,' Sheena remarked as Anna yawned.

'I think I'll go have a lie-down and get the boys to have a rest. If I'm not up when you leave, may I just say that it was lovely meeting you and your girls, Sheena.'

'Thanks. It was wonderful to meet you, too,' she said, smiling brightly.

'Would you mind if we popped into the hospital to visit? I'd love you to meet my husband and my eldest boy. He'll be sorry he missed meeting you all.'

'Of course. I'd be delighted.'

Anna nodded and headed off just as Will brought Sheena a cup of tea. He set it down on the table before sitting next to her, putting his arm about her shoulders as she continued to feed Sarah.

'Ellie's sound asleep,' he said, glancing over to where his mother was reclined in her chair, Ellie asleep with her head on Mary's shoulder. 'And Dad's eager to have another hold of Sarah once you've finished feeding her.'

Stephen had gone off to help Anna settle her two boys but had already promised to return for another cuddle with Sarah. 'They really love children, don't they?' she said.

'Absolutely. They're very involved with their grandchildren and helping out my siblings whenever they need them.'

Sheena turned to look at him. 'They're amazing people, Will. You're so blessed to have them.'

'*We* could be blessed together, Sheena. The four of us. You, me, Ellie and Sarah.'

Sheena swallowed over the lump in her throat. 'A family?'

'Yes.'

'But, Will… what if I can't have any more children? You deserve to have more, to be a hands-on dad just like your own father and be involved in your children's lives. I can't give you that prom—'

Will leaned over and kissed her mouth. 'You taste so sweet, so perfect,' he murmured against her mouth, breaking away for a second so both of them could drag in a breath.

'It's always like this when I'm with you. So powerful. So perfect,' she added, her words breathless as she leaned towards him, eager to have his mouth on hers once more. He didn't disappoint her but he did manage to slow it down a little, to ease the frenzy of the kisses both of them seemed to need so desperately.

She was close. His mouth was on hers, his tongue tracing the edge of her lips, tasting her, tantalising her to distraction. She moaned a little sigh against him and sank deeper into his arms. He held her close, thrilled at the way she was responding to him, elated that he could still affect her in such a way and delighted that he'd been handed a second chance to do so.

'You can't always kiss me into submission every time I'm saying something you don't agree with,' she murmured, trying not to disturb Sarah, who was almost asleep as she finished feeding.

'Why not? Don't you enjoy it?' He waggled his eyebrows up and down suggestively, and she smiled at him and shook her head.

'Put your arrogance away and be serious. What if I—?'

A loud, ear-splitting scream filled the air, piercing their quiet solitude, cutting off what

Sheena had been about to say. After the scream came an almighty crash, as though a car had just driven through the front of the house.

Will sprang to his feet, heading in the direction of the noise. Sarah jumped, then pulled away, spluttering and crying at being disturbed. Sheena quickly buttoned her top and by the time she'd shifted Sarah to her shoulder and then stood, Mary was by her side, arms opened wide to receive the babe.

'Ellie's still asleep. I've put her in the pram,' the experienced grandmother said.

'Jesse? Jesse?' They could hear Anna calling throughout the house and a moment later Lester's cries filled the air as the baby woke from his sleep because of the commotion.

'Give me Sarah and go and see if Will needs help. Stephen will look after Lester.'

Sheena nodded and handed her grizzling daughter to Mary. Will was moving through the four-bedroomed house like lightning, opening and closing doors to check that everything was all right…until he came to Stephen's study.

'The door's jammed shut,' he said when he saw Sheena in the hallway.

'Jesse?' Anna came into the hallway from one of the rooms where she'd put Lester down for a nap. 'Where's Jesse?' She was as white as a sheet. 'He fell asleep with me on the bed but he's not there. Will?' Anna was starting to panic as Will and Sheena tried to push open the door to Stephen's study.

'It's jammed,' Will said. 'Something is blocking the way.'

'We'll have to get in through the window,' Sheena said. She could hear Sarah still crying in the front room and Mary singing to her. Lester was crying in one of the nearby bedrooms and Stephen was attempting to calm his grandson down. Anna looked so pale that Will quickly helped her to sit on the floor.

'We'll find him. We'll sort everything out,' he reassured his little sister, before heading outside to get a ladder. Sheena stood in the hallway, and the noise surrounding her started subsiding. She heard a small whimper coming from Stephen's study.

'Jesse?' she called with calm authority. 'Jesse? Can you hear me?'

Another whimper was her only reply but it was proof that he was in there and as they were unable to open the door, it was logical to surmise that something had fallen down, pinning Jesse and blocking the doorway.

'Jesse, I want you to stay very still. OK? Just like a statue. Uncle Will and I are coming to get you.'

'Jesse? Jesse?' Anna was panicking and there was the hint of mild hysteria in her tone. Sheena instantly turned to face the young mother.

'Anna.' She placed her hands reassuringly on Anna's shoulders, trying to calm her down. If Jesse heard the panic in his mother's voice, it might make him more upset and he could do things that could cause him further damage, especially if he was pinned under something heavy. 'He's in there. I can hear him. My guess is that he's trapped beneath whatever is blocking the door but it's of the utmost importance that we keep him calm and still until Will can get to him. You can speak to him but you *must* remain calm and controlled.'

'Yes. Yes.' Anna tried to breathe in and out more slowly. Stephen appeared in the hallway a moment later, a pink-cheeked, wet-eyed Lester in his arms.

'Sheena!' Will called from the front of the house. 'Sheena, I need you out here.'

'Coming,' she called, then turned to look from Stephen to Anna. 'Jesse needs to stay calm and still. Just talk to him, let him hear your voices. Reassure him.'

'Right you are, Sheena,' Stephen replied, nodding wisely. Sheena quickly headed out the front door, where she found Will positioning a small stepladder near the partially open front window, which was situated a metre and a half from the ground.

'I can't get it open too far due to the locks on the window but it should be wide enough for you to squeeze through,' Will said.

'OK.' She instantly climbed the ladder, glad she'd decided to wear trousers instead of a skirt, and shifted sideways, putting her foot up on the window ledge. Pushing aside the curtains, she shimmied and squeezed her way through the small gap, almost getting stuck a few times and knocking over something that had been positioned near the window, but within a few minutes she was through.

'The bookshelf has come down,' she called as she turned and unlocked the window from the inside so that Will could push it open the rest of the way and climb through to help her. 'Jesse? It's Sheena. Uncle Will's friend. Just stay still, sweetheart,' she called calmly, still unsure exactly where the little boy was.

'Good heavens!' Will said as he climbed through the window, almost tripping over a mountain of books on the floor. 'Dad. I'm going to need your help in lifting this bookshelf.' Will spoke in a tone that was calm and controlled yet the hint of urgency was evident in what needed to be done.

'Right you are, son,' came Stephen's calm voice.

'What's happening?' Anna said from the other side of the door. 'Is he all right? Jesse?'

At the sound of his mother's voice, another whimper sounded from beneath the pile of rubble and Sheena quickly scrambled in that direction. Within several seconds Stephen was through the window and into the room, both he and Will shifting around to position themselves on either side of the large wooden bookcase.

'Can you see him?' Will asked, almost ready to lift.

'I think I can see his foot. See? Just there.' She pointed to an area in the middle of the room where she'd managed to shift a few of the books out of the way but couldn't do any more until the bookcase had been lifted away.

'Yes. Good. It's all right, Anna. We'll have him out in a jiffy,' Will called reassuringly to his sister. Sheena could hear the love and reassurance in his tone and her heart swelled with pride for this man. He was so good, so caring, so loving to those around him. He was *her* Will. She didn't want to let him go, not ever, but… could they work things out? Would he be happy with only Ellie and Sarah? Two girls who weren't biologically his children?

Will looked over at his father and nodded once, the two men not needing any other words to communicate what had to happen next. Together they hefted the large bookcase out of the way and instantly Sheena scrambled to where Jesse lay buried beneath the books and papers that had been in the bookcase, pushing them out of the way in order to get to the little boy.

'There you are. Keep still. You're all right,' she murmured, desperate to reassure the little boy as her hands felt over his limbs, checking his body. Once the bookcase was upright and out of the way, Stephen opened the door to let Anna in while Will came and knelt down on the other side of his nephew.

'How is he?'

'Check his right leg for me,' she instructed as she pressed her fingers to Jesse's carotid pulse. 'Hey, there, Jesse. Can you hear me?'

Her answer was a whimper but the little boy didn't open his eyes. 'Pulse is strong. Breathing is good. Bit of a lump on his head where it connected with the shelf.' She lifted his eyelids to check his pupils and he whimpered and turned his head away, moaning, more in annoyance than in pain. 'Ahh…we have cognitive function.'

'Oh, Jesse. Jesse. You scared Mummy,' Anna said as she rushed into the room, almost tripping over the paraphernalia that was littered about the place, but Stephen was by her side, steadying his pregnant daughter. Mary stood in the doorway with a quiet Sarah securely in her arms, Lester clinging to her leg.

'Don't touch him just yet,' Will said when it appeared Anna was ready to scoop her boy up into her arms. 'Just let Sheena and I make sure he's OK. Almost done.'

'I'm so glad the two of you were here,' Mary murmured. 'See, Anna? No one better than two trained doctors and one of them your big brother to help out and take care of Jesse. It'll all be fine.'

'Although it does appear he may have broken his leg,' Will told his sister. 'I'll need to see an X-ray to confirm it but—'

'What? An X-ray? Is it that bad? Will he need to go to hospital?' Anna started to breathe more heavily and Sheena instantly looked at the expectant mother, concern for Anna's blood pressure now starting to worry her. 'I need to call Jeff. He needs to know what's happened. Oh, my poor Jesse. A broken leg. X-rays. Hospitals.'

'He's fine, Anna. Fine. Just a broken leg and as I'm an orthopaedic paediatrician, I'm the perfect person to look after him. He'll be just fine,' Will reiterated. 'Mum, do you have any children's paracetamol? Or ibuprofen?'

'Can you give ibuprofen to a child his age?' Anna asked.

'You can if you're an orthopaedic paediatrician and know the correct dosage,' he returned, and winked at his sister. 'I'm here, Anna-banana.' At the use of the childhood nickname, his sister gave him a watery smile. It was the most perfect thing he could have done. 'I'm not going to let anything happen to my precious nephew.'

'Come on, love,' Stephen said, helping his daughter to her feet. 'Let's give Will and Sheena some room. Come and sit down and put your feet up. We don't want your blood pressure rising too far.' Stephen looked at his son before he left, mouthed the word 'Ambulance' and received a nod from Will.

A moment later Mary returned, minus Sarah and Lester, who were apparently now with Stephen, bringing not only medication but some bandages as well. Jesse had opened his eyes but was more than content to lie still and have everyone make a fuss of him. Sheena took the bandages and searched around for something stable to act as a splint.

'What were you doing in Grandpa's study?' Mary asked him softly as she bent over him and kissed his cheeks. Will administered the medicine, knowing it wouldn't take too long to take effect.

'I wanted da big book. Da one with all the pictures of the horsies.' Jesse told his grandma. 'It was berry high up and I climbed and I climbed and then it was stuck.'

'You should have come and asked a grown-up to get it for you,' Mary scolded lightly, and Jesse's eyes began to tear up.

'I sorry, Grandma,' he said, and within a moment was crying, although Sheena had the feeling it was more because he was upset at having disappointed his grandmother than because of any pain. Carefully, Sheena and Will applied the splint and bandage to Jesse's right leg.

'How are you feeling now, little man?' Will asked his nephew.

'Am I still in trouble?' he asked softly, reaching for Sheena's hand and holding it tight. She smiled at his words as Will lovingly shook his head.

'No, matey. You're not.'

'Then I feel better,' he confessed, and Sheena couldn't help but laugh, the action helping to release her concern. It also made her wonder what the rest of her life was going to be like, being a mother to two small girls.

'One day Ellie and Sarah are going to be three years old, just like Jesse,' Sheena mused out loud, shaking her head as though she couldn't quite believe that day would come. 'How am I ever going to cope?'

Mary chuckled. 'You'll do fine. You simply take each day at a time and deal with whatever life throws at you. Never borrow trouble.'

Will was pleased with his mother's sensible advice but he could hear the depth of Sheena's words. 'You do realise that where Jesse is one little boy trying to get a book down from a bookshelf, you'll have two little monkeys getting into mischief. Double the trouble.'

'And from what I've seen, Sarah will be the one to lead the charge,' Mary added as she headed out of the room to check on everyone else.

Sheena shook her head in bemusement. 'It's so hard to imagine. Both of them running around, doing their own thing.'

'Living their lives like normal little girls.' Will smiled and reached over, taking her free hand in his and giving it a squeeze.

'Normal and filled with mischief.' Uncertainty gripped Sheena's heart and she bit her lip, unsure what her future held. 'What have I got myself into?'

Will chuckled before brushing a kiss to her lips. 'A whole world of love and laughter.' Which he was determined to share with her.

They stayed beside Jesse, making sure he didn't move until the ambulance arrived.

'Hey, Sheena. Hey, Will,' Dieter, one of the paramedics from Adelaide Mercy, greeted them. 'What are you two doing here?'

'This is my nephew,' Will explained, and as he and Sheena went to stand to give the paramedics some room, Sheena found her hand gripped firmly by Jesse.

'Stay,' he whimpered, and she could hear the panic behind his words.

'Of course I'll stay with you, sweetie,' she reassured him, and helped the paramedics transfer Jesse to the stretcher. Even when he was secure in the ambulance, Jesse still refused to let go of her hand and Sheena knew she'd have to stay with him. Her mind raced ahead, thinking of Sarah and Ellie.

'You'll need to go in the ambulance if he's not

going to let go of your hand,' Will pointed out as he came and sat beside her in the rear of the vehicle.

'I realise that because it's important to keep Jesse as calm as possible. Would you mind taking care of the girls? Driving them back to the hospital? I can meet you there.'

Will tried not to let his jaw drop at her words. 'You…trust me that much? You'll entrust your girls to my care?'

Sheena leaned over and kissed him. 'Of course I trust you. You *love* my girls. That much is quite clear to anyone who watches the three of you together. You honestly love them, Will, with all your heart, and I know you'll always protect them and keep them safe.'

He swallowed once, twice before answering. 'I will.' His tone was husky but it was also laced with determination. 'Right, then. I guess I'll see you back at the hospital.' He kissed her once more before saying goodbye to his nephew and climbed from the ambulance so that Dieter could shut the rear doors.

As Will watched the ambulance depart, he

couldn't believe the gift Sheena had just given him. Complete and utter trust for her daughters. Sheena could see how much he loved Ellie and Sarah. She could see that he wanted to protect those little girls for ever and she was willing to let him do it. She was willing to let him into her life and that was the biggest gift of all.

He'd let her down in the past. He realised that now. He hadn't spent the time to really get to know her, to understand the upbringing she'd endured, how sad and lonely she'd been. He'd been so wrapped up in finding the woman he wanted to spend the rest of his life with, so happy that he'd get to have his picture-perfect fairy-tale life that he hadn't *seen* Sheena for who she was deep down inside.

Since he'd returned to Australia and spent more time with Sheena, and her girls, he'd come to discover how sad and lonely she'd been all her life. He understood now why she'd never talked about her past or her endometriosis, but back then he'd only considered his own happiness and had blamed her when she'd turned his proposal down.

He'd let her down in the past but as he headed into the house to care for her beautiful daughters, he vowed that he wouldn't let her down again.

CHAPTER ELEVEN

WHEN they arrived back at Adelaide Mercy, Sheena handled Jesse's care, requesting X-rays to see if the little boy had sustained a greenstick fracture. Anna arrived just as Jesse was being wheeled to Radiology and finally the little boy was more than eager to let go of Sheena's hand when he had his mother right beside him.

'Hi, Sheena,' the triage sister said with surprise as she walked into the nurses' station where Sheena was writing up Jesse's notes. 'I didn't know you were scheduled for a stint in A and E today.'

'I'm not.' Sheena smiled and quickly explained about Will's nephew Jesse.

'So…where are the girls?' Sister was clearly puzzled.

'Will's bringing them back to the hospital.' Sheena looked at the clock on the wall. 'In fact, they should be back by now. Perhaps he's getting them settled in their room. It's been a big day. Do you mind if I use the phone to ring the ward and check?'

'Go ahead,' Sister remarked, a secret smile touching her lips. 'You and Will seem to be very close. At least, that's the impression we all have from the photo in today's paper.'

'Paper?' Sheena turned with the receiver to her ear and accepted the cut-out picture Sister offered. It was one of the photographs from the other day in the park when the photojournalist had caught them out, although it wasn't one of the ones they'd posed for. Instead, the paper had decided to go with the photograph of the babies in the pram, Sheena and Will sitting on the blanket, Will raising her hand to his lips. She read the caption below.

Sheena Woodcombe, mother of Adelaide's newly separated conjoined twins Ellie and Sarah, finds a quiet moment for romance with lead orthopaedic surgeon Will Beckman in the botanical gardens.

Sheena stared at it, stunned that she seemed to be some sort of celebrity and that people were interested in her love life.

'So I guess this means there *is* something going on between you and Will?' Sister fished. 'Is it serious?'

'As a heart attack,' Will remarked as he walked towards them. Sister quickly cleared her throat and returned to her duties as Will stared at the piece of paper Sheena held in her hands. She turned to face him and replaced the phone receiver in its cradle.

'You're here. Where are the girls?'

'All tucked up in their beds. Aunty Nessa is more than content to stand there and watch them sleep.'

Sheena sighed and smiled up at him. 'Good. Thanks for taking care of them.'

'No problem. Where's Jesse?' he asked as he took the picture from her fingers.

'Radiology.'

'You look great in this picture. It's definitely not my best side, though.'

Sheena chuckled. 'You're so vain.'

Will put his head on the side and looked at her. 'You don't mind about this?'

Sheena slowly shook her head. 'Not really. Perhaps before today I would have had a bit of a rant and rave about the media but…I don't know, today has changed things. Brought perspective.'

'Really? In what way?'

'In the way that a little boy climbing on a bookcase and hurting himself could have been a lot worse. In the way that families care and interact and show love for each other. In the way that even though I feel I'm floundering in a sea of parental confusion, everything will turn out right in the end. The media can take photographs and print what they like. They don't know the *real* story behind that moment. They don't know *me* and they probably never will. My girls are no longer conjoined and therefore no longer high-profile news. They're going to be able to grow up and enjoy normal lives. The past belongs in the past.'

She smiled and sighed as she said the words. 'And it feels great to say all of that out loud.'

Will nodded and reached for her hand. 'Come with me.'

'But I'm waiting for Jesse to return from Radiology,' she said as Will led her from the nurses' station.

'Call Dr Woodcombe in Paediatrics when Jesse returns, please,' he instructed the triage sister as they walked past. He was quiet as they took the stairs up to Paediatrics, walking along the busy corridors until they were back in Ellie's and Sarah's room.

'Janessa, would you mind waiting outside for a moment? I just need to propose to Sheena,' Will remarked, his words and tone direct.

'Uh? What? Uh…sure. Whatever you say,' Janessa said, as Will's words penetrated the haze around their friend. Janessa headed out of the room and closed the door behind her.

'You're proposing?' Sheena asked as both of them peered into the cribs, smiling at the two little girls, who were sleeping soundly.

'I thought I'd give you a heads-up this time so I didn't take you completely by surprise.'

'Very considerate of you.' She couldn't help the

wide beaming smile on her face. He was going to propose? Really? Her heart rate picked up as her mind processed the information but she forced herself not to jump ahead with a million and one questions, but instead to relax and focus on the moment.

He crossed to the vase that held the freesias he'd brought her that morning and plucked one out before turning to face her. He twirled the bloom in his fingers.

'I hope this goes better than last time,' he murmured with a slight frown.

'It will,' she replied encouragingly.

'Oh. Good. That certainly gives me a confidence boost.' He cleared his throat and took one small step towards her. 'I love you.'

'Strong beginning,' she whispered, her heart leaping with joy at hearing those words from his lips.

'Shh.'

'Yes. Of course. Sorry.' She nodded once. 'Please. Continue.'

Will laughed then took another step towards her. 'I have always loved you, Sheena, and I am so grateful that you've been able to have children and that those children were conjoined and that I was asked to come and look after them. The past belongs in the past. Hearing you say those words made me realise that you were right.

'It's the future we should be concerned about. The girls' future—*our* future—and I want that future to start right now. I love your girls, Sheena. I love them with every beat of my heart and I will continue to love them for the rest of my life. And, yes, before you ask, I would love to have more children but not at the expense of your health.

'*You* are far more important to me than the possibility of having more children. We have two beautiful girls and they'll fill our life with so much sunshine we'll need to wear dark glasses.'

Sheena chuckled and then gasped as he took one last step towards her and slid his arm about her waist, drawing her close to him. As he pressed her body against his, she sighed with delight, her gaze taking in his gorgeous mouth for a moment before she looked deeply into his mesmerising blue eyes.

'Sheena.' Her name was a caress on his lips. 'Will you do me the honour of becoming my wife?' He handed her the single freesia as he spoke the words and she accepted it with a nervous smile.

Sheena swallowed and licked her suddenly dry lips. She was about to give her answer when Sarah started to fuss.

'And could you be quick with the answer because I think *our* daughter is about to wake up?'

Sheena's smile was as bright as the love in her heart. 'I can't believe this is actually happening. That I'm so fortunate to have you back in my life, to be able to contemplate a future with you. I love you, Will. So very much. And I'm the luckiest woman in the world to be able to have a strong, protective man like you to call my husband. I want to build a life with you and the girls. The four of us together as a family, and if any other children come along—the more the merrier. Thank you for loving my babies and wanting them to be your own. I'm honoured.'

Will's smile was dazzling as he lowered his head, claiming her lips in a kiss that held all the promise of a wonderful future together. In the background, they both heard Sarah's fussing turn to grizzles and in another moment those grizzles would turn into her cries for attention, and when those cries came, they would need to part to go and attend to her before she woke Ellie...but until then Will was more than content to kiss his new fiancée, their hearts forever joined with the purest love.

EPILOGUE

'QUIET. Quiet, please!' Giuseppe demanded as he walked through his restaurant, which was closed for a private function—the function being the first birthday celebration of Adelaide's first previously conjoined twins, Ellie and Sarah Beckman.

The restaurant had been decorated in blue, which was Sarah's favourite colour, and yellow, which Ellie had declared she loved. Frills and flowers and lace and soft toys in the chosen colour theme were placed around the room, making it feel more like a toy factory than a restaurant.

'Quiet. Quiet, please!' Giuseppe called again. 'The mother and the father want to propose the toast.'

The family and friends gathered to celebrate Ellie and Sarah's first birthday all shifted back to their seats. While the girls were too young to ever remember this day, Will had arranged for his father to film the proceedings. 'That way we can embarrass them on their twenty-first birthdays by replaying it,' he'd lovingly suggested to his wife.

Will stood, scooping Sarah into his arms, shifting her around so he could put his other arm around Sheena's shoulders. 'Thank you, Giuseppe,' he called as the noise died down. Sheena bent to pick up Ellie, the little girl resting her head on her mother's shoulder as she looked out at the crowd before them.

Miles and Janessa were standing not too far away, almost ready to leave for their next adventure—in the UK, looking after the next set of conjoined twins. They'd delayed their departure specifically to be here today. 'There's no way I'm missing my nieces' first birthday,' Janessa had declared, and Miles had readily agreed with her.

Anna, Jeff and the rest of their brood, along with a brand-new granddaughter for Mary and Stephen, sat not too far away. Kaycee, Raquel-

Maria, Clementine, Charisma and many of their other friends from the hospital were there as well, all smiling and beaming brightly at the two gorgeous little girls who had brought such happiness into their lives.

Two months ago Will had surprised Sheena with a glorious pre-wedding gift of a five-bedroom home with a large backyard only fifteen minutes from Adelaide Mercy. Both Will and Sheena had decreased their hours at the hospital in order to spend as much time with their girls as they could, the four of them bonding together in perfect harmony.

Will had applied to officially adopt the girls but in his heart they already were and always would be *his* sweet Sarah and *his* elegant Ellie. He cleared his throat and looked around the room at everyone who had come to celebrate with them, then his gaze settled on his wife.

His wife. *His* Sheena. He loved her more today than he had for the past ten years and he knew she felt the same way. They talked daily, about deep and meaningful things, about plans they had for their future.

She looked up at him and smiled brightly. 'I love you,' she said softly, before he bent and brushed a kiss across her lips.

'Love you right back,' he murmured. Their wedding two months ago had been a quiet affair held in the backyard of their new home. Intimate and relaxed, just the way they'd both wanted it, and two weeks ago, when the girls had finally been released from the hospital, their lives had begun in earnest.

'Friends,' Will began, feeling Sarah already impatient to be down and crawling around the floor, getting her pretty blue dress all dirty. He smiled. That was his girl. No doubt she'd have Ellie into all sorts of mischief before the evening was over and he looked forward to discovering what they would do next.

'Thank you all for coming to help us celebrate the first birthday of these two very special girls. Sheena and I had many things to say, many people to thank, but Sarah's eager to be down and enjoying herself once again so in order to acknowledge her impatience—no doubt for the incredible cake Giuseppe has created—please, all raise your glasses of milk as we toast Sarah and Ellie.'

'To Sarah and Ellie,' everyone toasted, clinking their glasses of milk and laughing.

Sarah squirmed once more in her father's arms and Ellie snuggled into her mother but as soon as Will put Sarah down, Ellie immediately erupted with energy and was eager to be off after her sister.

Will drew his wife close and pressed another kiss to her lips. 'We're going to have our hands full,' he said.

'Even fuller than we ever expected,' she murmured, her words punctuated with deep meaning. She eased back to look directly into his eyes. Just after their wedding, Sheena had needed to have two cysts removed from her ovaries, as well as be treated for her increasing endometriosis. Both she and Will had been told that if they wanted to try for more children, there was an extremely small window of opportunity, and until today, when Sheena had returned to see her surgeon for a review, she hadn't dared to hope for such incredible news.

Sheena smiled up at him, her heart bursting with love as she nodded, tears beginning to glisten in her eyes.

'What?' Will was stunned.

'I'm pregnant. I only found out an hour ago, and you were finishing up in surgery and then with coming here and… We're going to have a baby. The ultrasound is booked for tomorrow and I'll need to take things even easier and—'

Will pressed his mouth to hers in complete happiness. 'We're going to have another baby! I can't believe that we've been so blessed already with the girls and now we're—'

Sheena employed his tactic and kissed him quiet, knowing he wouldn't mind.

'We already have the fairy-tale family,' she murmured against his mouth. 'But this new baby will be the crowning glory.'

'And he will be loved and cared for as much as his big sisters,' Will announced with joy.

'He? Who said anything about it being a boy?'

Will winked at his wife. 'Trust me!'

* * * * *

Mills & Boon® Large Print
Medical

March

CORT MASON – DR DELECTABLE	Carol Marinelli
SURVIVAL GUIDE TO DATING YOUR BOSS	Fiona McArthur
RETURN OF THE MAVERICK	Sue MacKay
IT STARTED WITH A PREGNANCY	Scarlet Wilson
ITALIAN DOCTOR, NO STRINGS ATTACHED	Kate Hardy
MIRACLE TIMES TWO	Josie Metcalfe

April

BREAKING HER NO-DATES RULE	Emily Forbes
WAKING UP WITH DR OFF-LIMITS	Amy Andrews
TEMPTED BY DR DAISY	Caroline Anderson
THE FIANCÉE HE CAN'T FORGET	Caroline Anderson
A COTSWOLD CHRISTMAS BRIDE	Joanna Neil
ALL SHE WANTS FOR CHRISTMAS	Annie Claydon

May

THE CHILD WHO RESCUED CHRISTMAS	Jessica Matthews
FIREFIGHTER WITH A FROZEN HEART	Dianne Drake
MISTLETOE, MIDWIFE...MIRACLE BABY	Anne Fraser
HOW TO SAVE A MARRIAGE IN A MILLION	Leonie Knight
SWALLOWBROOK'S WINTER BRIDE	Abigail Gordon
DYNAMITE DOC OR CHRISTMAS DAD?	Marion Lennox

June

July

August